"Julia, I
to know
genuine.

She looked up, her eyes soft. "I don't know what to say. You've become an important part of my life."

"We can take things slow."

She nodded, lacing her fingers through his. "Can you give me some time? This thing between us is, um, unexpected."

"Sure. I'm not going anywhere."

Sean waited for her to start climbing the stairs before heading back along the path to his Jeep.

He drew in a deep breath. What had happened tonight? Their relationship had shifted to a different level, whether Julia was prepared to admit it or not.

He walked around to the driver's side of the Jeep, his step light. There had been an unexpected depth to their kiss, a strong emotional connection that he hadn't experienced before. The possibility of a future with Julia looked promising.

Narelle Atkins lives in Canberra, Australia, with her husband and children. Her love of romance novels was inspired by her grandmother's extensive collection. After discovering inspirational romances, she decided to write stories of faith and romance. A regular at her local gym, she also enjoys traveling and spending time with family and friends.

Books by Narelle Atkins

Love Inspired Heartsong Presents

NARELLE ATKINS

Winning Over the Heiress

HEARTSONG
PRESENTS

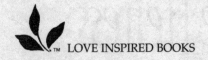 LOVE INSPIRED BOOKS

Recycling programs for this product may not exist in your area.

ISBN-13: 978-0-373-48769-1

Winning Over the Heiress

www.Harlequin.com

Printed in U.S.A.

He has saved us and called us to a holy life—
not because of anything we have done but because of
His own purpose and grace. This grace was given us
in Christ Jesus before the beginning of time.
                    —*2 Timothy* 1:9

For my husband, Jay, and my children, who provide unending love, encouragement and support. I love you.

Acknowledgments

I appreciate the help I've received from many people during the writing of this book. Susan Diane Johnson (Suzie Johnson) and Stacy Monson, my wonderful critique partners. Many thanks to Laura O'Connell for her insightful critiques on an earlier version of this story.

I thank my reader friends for their helpful feedback and support: Jen B, Lisa B, Raylee B, Karinne C, Tracey H, Daniela M, Heather M and Merlyn S.

A special thank-you to my editor, Kathy Davis, and the team at Harlequin.

Chapter 1

Julia Radcliffe signed on to the computer at the reception desk in the Beachside Community Church office, ready to start her workday by updating the member database. She tucked her auburn hair behind her ears and skimmed through the list of names, noting Cassie and Ryan Mitchell's new Queensland address. They had recently celebrated their first wedding anniversary in their new waterfront home, which came complete with a private mooring for Ryan's yacht.

An image popped into her head: Sean Mitchell, Ryan's brother, dressed in a tux at her best friend's wedding. Her face warmed at the memory of her encounter with Sean at the posh Sydney hotel. A year ago, he'd walked out on her at Cassie and Ryan's wedding.

Julia sipped the latte she'd picked up at a Manly café on her way to work. Cassie claimed Sean, her old friend and brother-in-law, had changed. Was it possible for someone with Sean's history to turn his life around that drastically in just eighteen months?

The phone rang, and she transferred the call to Simon, the assistant pastor. Simon was a great boss, and he'd helped her settle into her new office manager maternity-relief role. She was blessed to have the opportunity to work at her church and support the paid staff in their various ministries.

The automatic external sliding glass door opened. Liam, a guy she had dated last month, walked hand in hand through the reception area with a slender blonde girl.

Her stomach sank. No wonder he hadn't called her after their second date.

Liam approached her desk. She greeted him, pasting a polite smile on her face. "Can I help you?"

"Sally and I have an appointment with Simon at nine."

Julia nodded. "Please take a seat on the sofa. I'll let him know you're here." She picked up the phone handset, professionalism overriding her curiosity. When had they started dating—before or after Julia's second date with Liam a few weeks ago?

Simon didn't answer his phone, and she swallowed hard, realizing she'd dialed the wrong extension. She pressed the correct number and, in a calm voice, told Simon his next appointment had arrived.

Liam sat close beside the blonde. They seemed cocooned in their own little world, reading something together on his phone. He attended a different church, and had told Julia all about his plans for Bible college. Plans that now appeared to include his new girlfriend.

Julia slumped in her seat and logged back in to the database. Her French-manicured nails clicked on the keys as she entered Cassie and Ryan's new address. *Lord, will I ever meet my future husband? Should I quit dating and accept my lot in life as a single woman?*

She pressed Enter to accept the final changes in the database. Liam and the blonde were now in Simon's office. She glanced at the open sliding door, her pulse quickening.

Sean. What was he doing here? Dressed in a casual shirt and jeans, his gaze darted around the empty reception area before homing in on Julia.

She held her breath for a moment, catching the flicker of recognition lighting up his face. His hair had grown long. He looked like a surfer boy, with his golden tan and sandy locks that curled over his ears.

He stopped a few feet away from her desk. "Hey, Julia, I didn't know you worked here."

"I started only a couple of weeks ago."

His smile widened. "Is Simon around?"

"You know Simon?"

"Ryan introduced us at church recently."

"Oh, I didn't know you were attending services here." Sean had moved to Queensland with Ryan and Cassie not long after their wedding, and Ryan often travelled back to Sydney for work. Julia had chatted with Cassie on the phone last night, and she'd done her best to steer the conversation away from Sean.

His eyes, the exact color of the sky on a sunny day, sparkled. "I moved into Ryan's old apartment last week, and he suggested I come here."

"Okay." Maybe Cassie was right and Sean did share her faith now. A dramatic turnaround from his attitude and behavior at the wedding. "Simon's in a meeting, and he shouldn't be too long."

"No problem." He remained standing by her desk.

She should tell him to take a seat—she had work to do—but her overflowing email account could wait. Why did she let his smile dominate her thoughts? She should be immune to his charm. "I love the harbor views from Ryan's apartment."

"Me, too. I can walk to the beach for my early-morning surf. Do you work here full-time?"

"Yes, I'm covering my friend's maternity leave, and right now there's more than enough work to keep me busy." Some days she wondered if she'd ever get through the backlog of admin work she'd inherited.

"I bet it's a nice change of pace from your stressful banking job in the city."

"It sure is. My last couple of personal-assistant roles at the bank were crazy busy all the time, so I resigned from the bank when I got this job."

"Really? That's a big decision if this job is only temporary."

"After eight years it was time for a change. I was only nineteen when I first started working there."

"That's a long time." Sean's phone beeped, and he checked the screen. "I'd better take a seat and let you get back to work."

She nodded, and swallowed the dregs of her tepid coffee. Her gaze kept wandering in Sean's direction as she checked her email. He flicked through a magazine, appearing more centered and relaxed than the last time she'd seen him.

Footsteps sounded in the hall, and Liam appeared with the blonde. She headed for the exit while Liam wandered to Julia's desk.

She squared her shoulders, waiting for him to speak.

"Um, I should have called you," Liam said.

"I can see you've been busy."

A tinge of red shaded his face. "You're a great girl, and you'll meet the right guy one day."

She groaned, her gaze sliding over to Sean.

Sean bent his head, studying an unopened magazine in his lap. He was close enough to hear every word.

She forced her mouth into a smile. "Well, then, I guess I should wish you all the best for Bible college."

"Thanks. Sally's waiting, I'd better go." Liam turned away and hurried out of the building.

Sean met her gaze, his lips twitching in the direction of a smile. "His loss. You're too good for him."

More heat invaded her flushed face. "Did anyone ever tell you it's rude to eavesdrop?"

He shrugged. "You're better off without him."

"You think so?"

"Yes." His voice dropped an octave, a teasing lilt matching the playful glint in his eyes. "You're way too good for him, but he's not smart enough to work it out."

Before she had a chance to respond, Simon appeared in the reception area. "Sean? I'm ready for you now."

Sean jumped out of his seat, and the two men walked together down the hall toward Simon's office.

Julia nibbled her lower lip. Sean's flattering words and perceptive assessment of the Liam situation had soothed her battered heart. What else could happen to surprise her today?

Already this morning she'd found a letter regarding her adoption inquiry in her mailbox. The search for her birth mom had officially commenced, after the government agency had misplaced her initial application a few months earlier.

Fear curled in her belly. She loved her adoptive parents and Billie, her adopted younger sister. Billie had talked her into tracking down the location of her birth parents. Billie was keen to meet her birth mother, but Julia didn't know if she was ready to meet the woman who had given her life. And then given her away.

Before long, Simon reappeared with Sean. She checked the time on her computer screen. What had they been discussing for the past hour? Not that it was any of her business. Instead, she should be thankful that Sean had found a church home.

"Have you taken your morning break?" Simon asked.

She shook her head. "I'm swamped with the news bulletin and website updates." Her web skills were limited and she struggled to do basic text updates, let alone anything more complicated.

"You won't have that problem for long," Simon said.

She lifted a brow. "Who else is going to do it?" The church had advertised a new position for a website administrator last month. To her knowledge, they hadn't found any suitable applicants.

Sean hung behind Simon like a shadow, checking out the office.

Simon smiled. "We have a plan, and I'll let you know what's going on when I bring back your latte and muffin."

"Thanks, that sounds great." She rummaged through her purse and handed over cash to Simon. They'd fallen into a routine of taking turns for the midmorning coffee run.

Simon left the building with Sean, walking outside into the sun-drenched paved courtyard.

She ran her fingers through her wavy hair, untangling a small knot. What was going on? It was as though Simon and Sean had become new best friends. Perplexed, she skimmed her email to see if she'd missed any news bulletin announcements.

Sean strolled beside Simon to the nearby café across the road, an energetic bounce in his step. His prayers for a new job had been answered this morning.

Simon halted at the pedestrian crossing. "Julia usually likes a tall latte with no sugar, although she occasionally wants a cappuccino. She likes her low-fat berry muffin heated, too. Blueberry is her favorite, followed by raspberry."

"Okay, is this part of my job description?"

Simon laughed. "No, but she's a hard worker, and we appreciate her willingness to fill the maternity-relief role. I assume you know Julia through Cassie."

"We met at Ryan and Cassie's wedding." Julia had captivated his thoughts since he'd first glimpsed her walking down the aisle in the church. She'd worn a stunning bridesmaid dress, the silky fabric gliding over her curves. Filtered sunlight through the stained glass windows had brought out the red highlights in her glossy hair and bathed her pretty face in a soft glow.

"Weren't you friends with Cassie years ago?"

Sean hung his head, distant memories of partying with Cassie leaving an unpleasant taste in his mouth. "Yes, but I met Cassie when I worked for her father's company, and Cassie didn't see much of Julia during that time."

"That makes sense."

Sean closed his eyes for a moment, thanking God he was a changed man and able to make amends for his past bad behavior. He'd made a number of enormous mistakes, leading to years of misery and heartache, which had culminated in a stint in a gambling rehab program not long before his brother's wedding.

The lights changed, and he crossed the road with Simon, welcoming this new chapter in his life. The opportunity to work with Julia was an unexpected bonus.

Fifteen minutes later, Simon and Sean returned to the church office. Julia spun around in her seat, thanking Simon for her latte and muffin.

The men pulled out chairs from under a nearby desk, making themselves comfortable.

Sean leaned back in his seat opposite her, cradling a small coffee cup in his hands.

"What's up?" She opened her muffin package and sipped her coffee, aware of Sean's intense scrutiny.

"I have some news," Simon said.

She swallowed a delicious piece of the warmed muffin, the sweet blueberry flavor lingering in her mouth. "Good news, I hope."

Simon smiled. "Sean's going to be working with us."

She gulped down a mouthful of coffee, the hot liquid scalding her throat. "You're kidding?"

Sean shook his head. "I start tomorrow."

She widened her eyes. "How's this going to work?"

"Sean's the successful applicant for the website admin job."

"Wow." She turned to Sean. "I didn't know you'd acquired IT qualifications."

Sean shrugged. "I have all the prerequisite skills needed for the job."

"Yes," Simon said. "He's also going to help you out with general admin and reception when you're super busy."

She slouched in her seat, her mind whirling. How had this happened? Why had the church chosen to employ Sean?

She sipped her latte, switching her attention back to Simon. "What hours will Sean be working?"

"He'll be here full-time. You'll be his supervisor."

No way. Her fingers trembled, and she placed her coffee cup back on her desk. All day, five days a week. Sean would be in her work domain. He'd be her responsibility to manage.

She pursed her lips, staring at the spare desk, less than ten feet away from her own. "And where will Sean be working?"

"Right here with you," Simon said. "We'll all feel

happier when we're out of the office, knowing Sean is with you."

She nodded, recalling the problems they'd experienced with a few rowdy visitors last week. "Do you want me to put aside the web updates for tomorrow?"

"Absolutely." Simon ate the last of his muffin and tossed the scrunched-up paper bag into a nearby trash bin. He stood. "I have a meeting in ten minutes I need to prepare for." He turned to Sean, his smile broad. "I'll see you at nine tomorrow."

Sean shook Simon's outstretched hand. "You sure will."

The assistant pastor headed down the hall toward his office, drinking his coffee.

Julia picked at her muffin. "Would you like a piece? I have plenty."

"No, I'm good."

"You won't be joining us in our coffee-and-muffin run?"

"Probably not." He stretched out his jeans-clad legs, his feet inches away from hers.

The phone rang and she excused herself to answer it. She handled the request from a church member, and swung back around to face Sean.

He drew his eyebrows together. "You didn't know I'd applied for the job? I'm surprised Cassie didn't tell you."

She shook her head. "Congratulations, by the way. Ryan and Cassie must be happy to see you settled."

"Actually, it was Ryan's idea I apply for this job."

"You didn't want to stay in Queensland?"

"Nope. There weren't any job vacancies in my field, and I couldn't work for Cassie at the resort, either."

She nodded. Cassie's father would veto any attempt by Cassie or Ryan to reemploy Sean in any of his companies. Sean had embezzled a large sum of money and disappeared, losing touch with Cassie and his family. A few years later, he had come out of hiding and they had discovered he'd taken the money to finance his gambling addiction.

"Ryan figured a church would be a good work environment for me."

"That's logical." She drank her latte, inhaling the comforting and familiar aroma. She should have guessed Ryan had lined up the job. Ryan and Cassie had done whatever they could to help Sean overcome his problems.

Sean rubbed his hand over his clean-shaven jaw, frown lines forming between his eyebrows. "Are you okay with this?"

"Of course." She studied her fingernails, putting on a brave smile. "An extra pair of hands will make my life easier."

Why did it have to be his hands? The unique scent of his earthy aftershave mingled with coffee surrounded her. How could she concentrate with him sitting close by all day?

He cleared his throat. "Why didn't you return my call?"

Her mouth gaped, and she was captured by his compelling gaze that demanded answers. "I was busy helping my sister move into my apartment, and you moved interstate a few weeks later."

"My phone number didn't change." He pushed a couple of unruly locks off his face. "Obviously I was wrong to think we could be friends—"

"No, that's not true." If only it were that simple.

He shook his head. "At the wedding, you were the one person who I thought understood me. You stood by Cassie when she was struggling to overcome her issues. I could have done with a friend last year."

She cringed, the intensity of his hurt smashing into her chest. She had let him down, like too many other people in his life. "I don't know what to say. You could have called me again…"

"And act like a stalker?" He laughed. "Another thing to add to my very long list of sins."

"Sean." She whispered his name and pressed her lips together. Now that they were working in close proximity and she was his boss, she needed to try to make this situation right. "I'm sorry. I know your extended family were less than pleasant at the wedding and gave you a rough time."

"That's an understatement."

"But you could have at least stayed at the reception until Ryan and Cassie left."

"You know why I had to leave."

"And you know why I had to stay." She stared into his eyes, pleading with him to understand her situation. "I was Cassie's bridesmaid. I couldn't abandon her. You were asking too much."

He held her gaze, his blue eyes softening. "I guess you're right."

"Sometimes we have to do things we don't like for the benefit of others. You should have stayed for the whole wedding to support Ryan and Cassie."

"I get that, and I didn't intend to put you in a difficult situation."

She nodded. "And I really couldn't see how I could help you from Sydney. I haven't even had a chance to visit Cassie in Queensland." Her unexpected and powerful emotional connection with Sean at the wedding had clouded her judgment. She'd balked at the thought of spending more time with him. And still did. Nothing had changed.

"Fair enough." He stood. "I'd better get going. I'll see you at nine tomorrow."

"I'll be here."

He winked and sauntered out the door.

She dropped her head into her hands. Her peaceful working life would never be the same.

Chapter 2

Sean checked the time on his phone as he raced into the church courtyard. Nine-fifteen. He was late for his first day at work.

He'd stopped outside the sports store up the road, despite knowing he was short on time. The Jet Ski he'd spotted in the window yesterday was on sale, and he'd salivated over the prospect of riding it in Sydney Harbour.

Sean shoved his hair back from his forehead, his heartbeat accelerating. Fallen leaves crunched underfoot, blown around the spacious courtyard by the tangy ocean breeze.

His financial situation wasn't great. *Dismal* was a more appropriate description. He couldn't afford to forget how much trouble he'd gotten into when he'd impulsively spent large amounts of money on credit. Or his foolish attempts to recoup the money by gambling and other reckless means. Ugh. If only he could erase the image of the sleek Jet Ski from his mind.

He slowed his pace at the entrance to the church office, inhaling a few deep breaths. Julia might be late this morning. He peered through the glass.

No such luck.

Julia sat behind her desk, her lustrous auburn hair hanging loose about her shoulders as she concentrated on the computer screen.

He stepped through the open sliding door into the reception area.

She frowned, glancing at the wall clock. "You're fifteen minutes late."

"I know. I'm sorry. I slept in and—"

She flicked her hand through the air, gold bangles jingling. "I don't need to hear your excuses. Please make sure it doesn't become a regular thing."

"Okay." The stony expression in her green eyes resembled a drill sergeant's. What had he gotten himself into with this job?

She stood and walked around her desk, her slender legs encased in black, tailored pants. Low heels adorned her petite feet.

He looked at his navy polo shirt and jeans. "Have I messed up on the dress code, too?"

She cracked a small smile, her gorgeous eyes softening. "I'm meeting my parents for lunch. They always insist on dining at their friend's posh harborside restaurant."

"The vegemite sandwich I packed this morning is sounding very ordinary compared to your lunch plans."

She laughed, adjusting the cuff of her pale blue silk shirt. "I do normally wear casual clothes to work."

"Right." He let out a big breath, liking the melodic tone of her laughter.

She pointed to the desk on the back wall. "You'll be working here, and I've put some of the website updates for this week in your in tray. I'll email the rest to you."

"Thanks." He threw his backpack under the desk. "Does anyone else use this computer?"

"Yes." She sat back in her seat. "The youth worker and the pastoral care worker, but they usually prefer to work in a vacant office or meeting room where they won't be interrupted."

"No worries." He adjusted the office chair and spun around to face her. If he stretched out his leg, he could tap her knee with his foot. The office seating arrangement was probably too cozy for her liking. "What do I need to get done today?"

"Thursday is news-sheet day." She grabbed a bundle of papers from her desk. "I'll get you to proofread these sheets for the different services, then we'll crank up the photocopier and start collating all the inserts for the news bulletins."

He glanced at the colorful A5 fliers. "How long does this take?"

She wrinkled her nose. "Too long when I don't have anyone helping me. The senior ladies hold a morning tea on Thursdays in the hall. We'll have quite a few visitors who'll drop in for a chat, slowing our progress."

"I guess it's best if you handle that side of things."

She grinned. "They're a sweet bunch, and they'll probably all think you're adorable. Don't worry. Smile and nod—you'll be all right."

He widened his eyes. "Maybe." Did she find him adorable? He wasn't convinced he'd cope well chatting with sweet old ladies. Especially if they were nosy and started asking questions about his past.

"I'll also teach you the phone system so you can look after the reception desk while I'm at lunch."

He nodded. "Is there a list of staff names somewhere?"

"Right here beside the phone on my desk." She pointed to a magenta spiral notebook. "You'll only need to know the extensions for John, our senior pastor, and Simon. By the way, Simon wants to meet with you after lunch to discuss plans for expanding the church website."

He smiled. "No problem. I'm looking forward to coding again."

She tilted her head to the side. "Whereabouts did you learn website design?"

He paused, wary of sharing too much information from his past. "Bali."

"Bali." She twirled a pen between her fingers. "Is that where you were hiding out a few years ago?"

He dropped his gaze. "Among other places. I lived in a beach shack, surfed and paid my way by building and maintaining websites."

"You took a course in Bali?"

He looked up. "An online course. I really enjoyed it. I discovered I liked playing around with websites."

She nodded, her eyes darkening. "It's good you learned a useful skill."

He crossed his arms over his chest. "I know what you're thinking." *Better to get this conversation out of the way sooner rather than later.*

"Really?" She curled a lock of hair around her finger. "And that would be…"

"I'm a changed man. Your petty-cash box is safe."

She lifted a well-groomed brow. "I'm trying to give you the benefit of the doubt. I guess time will tell."

"You can trust me." His gaze locked with hers. "I'm a hard worker, and I'll prove to you my faith has helped me to become a better person."

"Okay, then." Her cool tone belied her words.

His shoulders slumped. "You can't forget my past, can you? Did Cassie tell you what happened?"

She lowered her long lashes, studying her fingernails. "Cassie is my best friend. We've been friends since school. We tell each other pretty much everything."

"Oh." He ran his hand through his hair, staring at the beach landscape print on the wall. "I'm not proud of some of the things I did a few years ago. I'm trying to put it all behind me."

She nibbled her lower lip. "I realize this. I can see you're different compared to when I first met you."

He nodded. "I'm working through a program, and I rely on my faith to help me get through the day. It often isn't easy, but I do what I've got to do."

"I've been praying for you."

He lifted his chin. "You're serious?" This was the last thing he'd expected to hear. She hadn't forgotten about him after the wedding.

The corners of her mouth turned up in a hint of a smile. "Ryan and Cassie are proud of the progress you've made."

"Do you think we can work together every day?"

"If you're true to your word and work hard, everything should be fine."

It was all up to him. His actions would determine whether or not he was successful in this job. Ryan had offered him a lifeline, and he must do his best to make this opportunity work. Both Ryan and Simon had put their faith in him. He needed to live up to the task.

Insecurities plagued Sean, eroding his fragile self-confidence.

He squashed them, determined to ignore any negative thoughts. He could do it. This time, he wasn't going to mess up. This time, he had his faith to give him strength and hope.

He prayed God would carry him through each day and keep him on a steady path. His life depended on it.

Julia located her parents in the restaurant sitting beside an enormous floor-to-ceiling window. She strode across the busy dining room toward them.

Her parents waved as she approached their white-linen-covered table.

She smiled, looking forward to catching up with them over a short lunch. After reprimanding Sean this morning for being tardy, she didn't want to be late back from lunch.

Julia greeted her parents and slid into a vacant seat, her gaze sweeping over the sailboats anchored in the harbor.

"I'm so glad you could make it, dear," Frances said.

"I can't stay long."

Her father nodded. "I've already ordered your favorite prawn salad."

"Thanks, Dad."

"Billie couldn't make it for lunch," her mom said, "but she'll meet you at the church at five."

"No problem." Billie worked in a Manly podiatry clinic, and often cancelled lunch engagements at short notice if her morning appointments ran late.

Frances furrowed her brow. "Billie mentioned you received the letter."

"Oh." Julia tucked her hair behind her ears. "I was going to tell you about it over lunch."

"Did they say how long the search would take?" her mother asked.

She shrugged. "Who knows? They may even lose my application again."

Her mom, more so than her dad, had been struggling with her and Billie's quest to find their biological parents.

Bruce shook his head. "Bureaucracy runs amok again. The process isn't easy for you, sweetheart."

"I may come up empty, if my birth parents chose to remain anonymous."

Frances blinked, moisture gleaming in her hazel eyes. "Honey, I wish there was something I could do to help."

A waiter arrived with Julia's prawn salad and a sea-food platter for her parents.

She sipped her ice water. "Mom, no one will ever be able to replace you in my life. You know that."

"I knew the day would come when you and Billie would choose to search for your birth parents. I didn't re-alize it would be this hard." She dabbed her eyes with her linen napkin. "I'm sorry, I'm ruining everyone's lunch."

Her father reached across the table and held her moth-er's hand. "It's okay. I'll say grace and we can focus on enjoying our lunch."

Julia closed her eyes and listened to her dad's words. She was blessed to have two parents who loved her and had encouraged her to grow in her faith.

Yet a part of her yearned to know the people who had brought her into the world, to discover her genetic back-ground and learn if she had brothers, sisters or an ex-tended family she'd never known.

Julia opened her eyes and gave her mom a bright smile. "Whatever happens, you'll always be my mom and I'll still love you."

"I know." Frances lowered her lashes and picked up her cutlery. "I just want my precious girls to be happy."

"We'll be fine," she said, voice shaking. New doubts about the wisdom of her search filled her mind.

Julia sampled a bite of her prawn salad, savoring the fresh, salty flavor. "This tastes better than I remember."

"You should try the lobster next time," her dad said.

"Maybe I will."

Julia arrived back at the church office after lunch with one minute to spare.

Sean looked up from her desk, surrounded by half a dozen elderly church ladies talking in loud voices.

He blinked a few times. "I'm glad you're back."

She nodded, suppressing a giggle. "Hi, ladies. I thought you'd all be at lunch by now."

Mrs. Smith picked up her maroon purse off the edge of the reception desk, her wrinkled hands fiddling with the clasp. "The senior's special at the club finishes at two, and we thought we'd get acquainted with Sean since he's new."

Sean's eyes pleaded for Julia's assistance.

"You know, it's time for him to have lunch. We don't want him to run late for his meeting with Simon this afternoon."

Mrs. Smith's watery eyes gleamed. "Yes, dear, we wouldn't want to get him into trouble. We'll see you both next week."

He nodded. "We'll be here."

The ladies took their leave, and Sean exhaled a big sigh. "Are they always this, um, chatty?"

"It depends. You'll be a novelty for a few weeks. Did they mention their unmarried granddaughters?"

"Aha. It all makes sense now. You did warn me."

She laughed. "I can tell you the names and vital statistics for all their bachelor grandsons. Have you been attending the morning service?"

He nodded. "They remembered me."

"Then it might be a good idea to attend the evening service for a while. Until the dust settles and all."

"Do you go to the evening service?"

"Yes, and I help out with the younger youth group on Sunday mornings."

"That's good. Other than the ladies hanging around, nothing much happened while you were at lunch."

"I'm glad. You need to take your hour for lunch now, and Simon should be ready to see you when you get back.

I'm pretty sure he has allocated at least a few hours for your meeting."

"Okay." Sean grabbed his backpack. "Can you let Simon know I'll be in the lunchroom if he needs to see me earlier?"

"Sure thing. Enjoy your vegemite sandwich."

"I will." He waved goodbye and disappeared down the hall.

Julia wheeled her chair back to her desk and tidied up her work area. Thanks to Sean's help this morning, she was way ahead of her schedule and ready to start collating the first batch of Sunday news bulletins.

She lined up the multicolored piles of paper in order and started folding the news sheets.

Later in the afternoon, she pulled the final ream of printed paper out of the photocopier. The news bulletins were done. All she had left to do tomorrow was sort the lesson materials for the Sunday-morning children's programs.

She checked her watch. Billie should be here in five minutes. She'd hardly seen Sean since lunch. He'd been holed up in Simon's office, and she'd liked having the office space to herself again.

Minutes later, Billie breezed through the door.

"Hi, Jules," Billie said. "Did you have a nice lunch with Mom and Dad?"

"It was okay, except for when Mom got upset about our adoption search. Why did you have to say something?"

"Because you probably would have chickened out on telling them like you did last time."

Julia frowned. "I hate to see Mom upset."

"She's worried she'll lose us," her sister said. "As if we'd abandon her and run off with our biological mothers."

"Next time, can you please let me tell Mom my news in my own time?"

Billie lifted a brow. "It's no big deal."

"It is to Mom."

"She'll get over it. Dad's not too phased by it all."

Dad and Billie had a pragmatic streak their emotional mother lacked. Julia sometimes wondered if Billie took anything seriously. Or maybe she buried her feelings so she could live in denial and not be forced to face anything. What would happen if Billie's search for her biological parents didn't yield the result she wanted?

Julia called Simon to tell him she was leaving for the day. She collected her purse, then followed Billie out the door.

Billie gave her a conspiratorial smile. "How's it going working with surfer boy? He's easy on the eyes, that's for sure."

She elbowed her sister in the ribs. "Don't say that. Someone might overhear you and get the wrong idea."

Billie laughed. "You need to chill. I wouldn't mind working all day, every day, with someone like him."

"It's not as great as you think." Julia refused to admit that Billie might be right. Her sister didn't know the details about Sean's ugly past. If Billie knew the truth, she wouldn't be encouraging Julia to think of him as a romantic prospect.

"Cassie has great taste in men," Billie said. "Are you sure there isn't another cute brother hiding away somewhere?"

"You've seen the wedding photos."

"I'm a bit disappointed I wasn't able to meet him in the flesh today. Does he look as good in person as he does in the photos? I'll have to drop in on you at work soon to check him out."

"You're impossible." Julia walked up the ramp in the multistory parking lot. She pulled the keys to her late-model Honda out of her purse. "Let's go home, get changed and hit the gym."

"I'm in." Billie smiled. "Is that cool boxing class on tonight?"

Julia nodded. "It's just what I need." She could punch and kick out all her nervous energy before turning around and doing another long day at work with Sean tomorrow. Maybe she needed to attend a boxing class every day.

Chapter 3

On Sunday night, Sean slipped into a vacant seat in the back row of the Beachside Community Church. He'd attended the evening service a couple of times, leaving as soon as the service finished.

Six months ago, he'd rediscovered his childhood faith. He found the sermons at this church, and Ryan and Cassie's church in Queensland, both challenging and thought provoking.

The reality and consequences of the unwise decisions he'd made in the past had slammed him hard in the chest. He'd hurt too many people, and he carried around the burden of his guilt in his heart.

The Bible talked about forgiveness, but he didn't deserve to be forgiven by anyone. He struggled to comprehend and accept God's forgiveness of his sins because he was unworthy of God's love and forgiveness.

Simon stood on the stage at the front of the church and welcomed the congregation to the service. The church was nearly full, with a large crowd of teens and young adults filling the rows of seats.

A few people had smiled and waved in Sean's direction, probably recognizing him from either the previous weeks or his new job in the church office. The service had a friendly atmosphere. One day he might consider taking the plunge and stay after the service for coffee.

Sean's attention, as usual, was drawn to the worship band. A young guy played lead guitar on a Gibson Les Paul. He didn't need to catch a glimpse of the guitar to recognize the Gibson by its rich, distinctive tone.

The words of the first song appeared on the overhead screen. An exquisite female voice rose above the music.

He stared at the singer on the stage, his jaw dropping.

Julia. Her silky hair flowed over her shoulders. Her body swayed with the beat of the music.

Wow. She sounded like a professional singer. He'd be surprised if she hadn't taken singing lessons. Her voice, pitch perfect, hit all the high notes. She soared with the congregation to the very end.

Simon returned to the stage and Sean dropped back into his seat, blown away. Julia was full of surprises. His fascination with her intensified.

She'd been professional in her attitude toward him at work, although he suspected she was uncomfortable having him around all day. He'd done his best to assist her with tasks like photocopying and collating the news bulletins, and she'd made an effort to thank him for all his help.

Sean stood during the next song, transfixed by the beautiful tone of her voice. And he couldn't ignore the Gibson. He dreamed about owning one and having the pleasure of playing it whenever he wanted.

He'd spent hours strumming on his old acoustic guitar, the one possession he treasured and had kept with him during his nomadic years of traveling. He loved his guitar and its therapeutic benefits. It had helped him find a little bit of peace and hope in the midst of his jumbled and often crazy life.

John preached a sermon on coveting. Sean wanted to close his ears and slide through a large hole in the carpeted floor. His desire for things he couldn't afford had created chaos in his life. The Bible verses that John quoted lingered in his mind. Somehow he had to let go of his love for material possessions and put all his trust in Jesus.

Oh, man, that was much easier said than done. For years, he'd struggled with discontent, never having enough money to own and do the things he wanted. In contrast, his brother, Ryan, had worked hard and earned more money than he could ever spend.

Sean rubbed his hand over his jaw. Could his love for Jesus overcome his love for the good life? Was his faith strong enough to prevent him from succumbing to his old coping mechanisms when life became tough and difficult situations arose?

The service ended. Sean found himself drawn to the musicians on the stage instead of the closest exit.

The half dozen band members stood around chatting. The owner of the Gibson smiled as Sean approached the group.

"Hey, I'm Matt," he said.

"Sean." He shook hands with the guitarist. "Great guitar you have there."

Matt nodded. "I saved up for months. Finally bought her last week. She plays like a dream."

"I know." Sean ran his fingertips along the sleek maple neck of the guitar. "I'd recognize a Gibson Les Paul anywhere."

"Do you have one?"

Sean shook his head. "A friend of mine, who I used to jam with, owned one."

"Would you like to have a turn?"

"Yeah, that'd be cool."

Sean put the guitar strap around his neck and borrowed a pick from Matt. The tune to "Johnny B. Goode" came to mind.

He strummed the guitar, and the cadence transported him to a different place. He'd love to own this beauty. He closed his eyes and let the music wash over him, cleansing him of any thoughts other than the exceptional sound of the guitar.

He plucked the final note and opened his eyes. The musicians around him began to clap.

Matt grinned. "Buddy, you should join the band. We could do with another lead guitarist."

Sean shook his head. "My old acoustic isn't up to the task, and I don't have an electric."

"You can use the church's electric guitar we keep out back in a storage room. Talent like yours shouldn't be hidden."

"I agree." Julia approached the group. "You sounded fabulous."

"Thanks," he said, touched by her compliment.

"Okay, that decides it," Matt said. "Sean, are you free on Tuesday nights?"

He smiled. "I could make that happen."

"We practice here in the church every Tuesday night for the following Sunday. We have a roster system set up, and you won't have to play every week. Even once a month would be a great help."

Sean nodded. "I'm working in the church office. You can let me know the details. I'll see what I can do."

Matt smiled. "Too easy. Practice starts at seven sharp."

"Great," Sean said. "I'll catch you later."

He ambled away from the band.

"Hey." Julia caught up with him. "That was incredible. I had no idea you were such a talented musician." Her eyes softened.

His face grew warmer and he held her gaze. "And I had no idea you were such a gifted singer."

She laughed. "Thanks. Now let's go have coffee, and I'll introduce you to everyone."

"Okay." He was delighted to have the opportunity to spend more time with Julia. He looked forward to hearing her sing when he played guitar. Beautiful music would be the outcome, and he couldn't wait to attend a music practice with her.

Two days later, Julia raced into the church less than a minute before music practice was due to commence. She'd met with her mother after work and tried to console her concerning her search for her birth mother.

Some days, she wondered if it was worth all the grief. But deep inside her heart, she had an undeniable yearning to learn the truth about her heritage.

"Hi, guys." Julia placed her purse on the floor next to a microphone stand.

"Glad you could make it," Matt said. "You had us worried for a minute."

"Sorry, I got caught up with my mom." She arranged her sheet music on a stand and turned around, searching the building for Sean.

He entered the sanctuary from the back room, holding an electric guitar and a music stand.

"Hi, Sean," she said.

"Hey." He smiled, the corners of his eyes crinkling.

Her cheeks warmed. Flustered, she adjusted the height of her music stand. Loose pages of sheet music scattered over the floor.

"Let me help." Sean crouched beside her, gathering up the paper and passing it to her.

"Thanks." She riffled through the pile of paper, rearranging the pages in song order. Frustrated by her clumsiness, she focused her full concentration on the unnecessary task. She'd spent most of her day at work with Sean. She should be immune to his distracting masculine presence by now.

Sean chatted with the other musicians and tuned his guitar. Julia sipped her water and listened to their guy talk. Sean's extensive knowledge about guitars surprised her. He played some licks as they set up the sound system. She recognized talent mingled with hard work.

Sean glanced at her. "Does this sound okay?"

"You sound great."

"Really?" He frowned. "It's been a while since I've regularly played an electric. Sunday was the first time in ages."

"I'd never have guessed."

"What are you doing after practice?"

She shrugged. "Not much. I've got lessons to prepare for my girls at youth group on Sunday, and Billie's making dinner as we speak."

"She's your sister, right? The dark-haired girl in the photo on your desk?"

She nodded. "My adopted sister. We confuse people because we look totally different from each other."

Matt rounded everyone up, and they started practicing the first song.

Julia switched her attention from Sean to the music. A tickle irritated her throat, making her miss a couple of the high notes.

They took a short break after the third song. "Are you okay?" Sean asked.

"My singing is bad tonight." She drank from her water bottle, the tepid liquid soothing her throat. "I hope I'm not getting sick, because the other singers aren't available this weekend."

"You'll be fine." Concern laced his deep voice. "And you sounded great on Sunday night."

"She did, indeed," Matt said. "Uh, Julia, I just found out I can't go to the upcoming charity concert."

Julia widened her eyes. "No! You need to be there with me. I can't do it alone. What happened?"

"I have to go up the coast to my grandma's birthday party that weekend. She's turning seventy. My family is organizing a big reunion."

"Oh." She chewed her lower lip. "What are we going to do? Cancel?"

Matt shook his head. "I think I have a solution. If Sean's available, he can play guitar instead of me."

"Play where?" Sean asked.

"Julia and I are supposed to be performing at a concert organized by the local churches to raise money for homeless people. Are you interested in filling in for me? I don't want to bail and let the organizers down."

Sean met her gaze. "What do you think? Do I play well enough for this gig?"

"Yes, of course. Matt wouldn't have asked you if he didn't think you could do a good job."

"Julia is right," Matt said. "Are you in?"

"Sure. Let me know the date and I'll get back to you."

Matt smiled. "Thanks, man. I owe you one. You can borrow my acoustic if you like."

"Okay. What songs are you doing?"

"Just one," Julia said. "'Amazing Grace.'"

He nodded. "I know the hymn."

Matt clapped his hands. "Great. I think this will work out just fine."

Yeah, right. Her stomach churned, her earlier anxiety over the charity event performance returning in full force. The concert crowd would be big, and she'd never sung solo in front of an audience that large.

She'd need to do a lot of practice with Sean before the big night. Good thing the concert wasn't for a couple of months or so. But practice would take place outside of their normal work hours. She couldn't avoid spending more time with Sean. Why did that thought bring a small smile to her lips? Despite everything, especially his past, she found Sean intriguing and fun to be with.

They were becoming friends—quickly—and she reined in her unruly thoughts. She was Sean's supervisor. They needed to maintain a professional relationship. Anything else wasn't an option.

A couple of days later, Julia packed the last of the plates and cutlery from her pasta dinner with Billie into the dishwasher. Her sister had dashed out the door after dinner to meet a friend at a local café.

Julia's cell phone vibrated in her pocket. She retrieved it and checked the caller ID. Cassie.

Her smile widened. "Hi, Cass."

"How are you doing?"

"Pretty good, except for a niggling sore throat." She wanted to go to sleep early tonight in the hope of recovering faster. The last thing Sean needed was for her to call in sick tomorrow and throw him into the deep end at work. And she wanted her voice to improve for Sunday night.

"Take it easy," Cassie said. "The reason I called is I booked the flights for the resort opening weekend."

"Great. How much do I owe you?"

"Absolutely nothing. This trip is on me."

"I'm more than happy to pay my way." She had plenty

of savings, plus a sizable trust fund from her grandparents, which she accessed only in an emergency.

"No, I insist. I can't wait to see you again."

"Me, too. Did you manage to book flights on the Friday night and Monday night, even though it's a holiday weekend?"

"I sure did." Cassie lowered her voice. "Now, here's the thing. I booked you and Sean on the same flights."

She paused. "Really?"

"Yep. Ryan and I thought it best since his parents changed their plans and are flying here earlier in the week."

"I'll be sort of babysitting Sean?"

"Not exactly. We figured it would be better if he traveled with someone rather than by himself."

"I thought you trusted him these days."

"We do, but the family feels more comfortable knowing he won't be traveling alone." Cassie sighed. "Is this a problem for you?"

"No, of course not. I work with him every day." And now she'd be seeing him during her holidays, in addition to the extra music practices for the concert.

"Excellent. I'll email the itinerary to both of you tonight. Ryan's parents will be happy that the arrangements have been finalized."

"Sure. I'm looking forward to catching up with you."

"Me, too. It's going to be a bit of a family reunion for me and Ryan. Laura and Greg plus my mom are hoping to be here, too."

"I'm glad you'll have the opportunity to see everyone." If only the idea of spending more time with Sean wasn't so appealing. It was a good thing he wasn't suitable boyfriend or husband material. At least she knew Cassie wasn't trying to set her up with Sean.

Somehow she'd get through the weekend, and not let herself fall for Sean's charm.

Chapter 4

The next morning, Julia finished typing the minutes from the weekly staff meeting. Sean was now responsible for expanding the church's social media presence.

She furrowed her brows. Where *was* Sean? It was after ten, and she hadn't seen or heard from him.

The main door slid open. Sean strolled in with Simon. Both men were clad in full-length wetsuits and held surfboards under their arms. So that was where he'd been.

Julia saved the computer file and stood, stretching her back muscles. "Was the surf up this morning?"

"The surf was awesome." Simon rested the tail of his surfboard on the floor. "We hung out with the guys in the water and shared a few good conversations."

Sean nodded. "He did all the talking and I surfed."

"I can't believe you get paid to surf," she said.

Simon grinned. "You can always come with us. My offer to teach you to surf still stands. That's if you're brave enough?"

She wrinkled her nose. "I'm happy to let you two play with the sharks without me."

"Always an excuse. I'll clean up now and catch you both later." Simon disappeared in the direction of the shower facilities.

Sean raised an eyebrow. "I didn't think you were scared of anything."

She lifted her chin, looking him straight in the eye. "I tried surfing, but it's not my thing."

"Okay, I'll be back at my desk after I shower."

"No problem. You have a pile of work waiting for you."

He swiped a wet curl off his face. "I'm going to stay late to catch up on my work."

"You don't need to. I was joking around with Simon."

"I'm not the one getting paid to surf, and I promise I'll complete all of my work today."

"Hopefully you'll be done by five."

"Yep. I'll see you soon." He disappeared down the same hall as Simon, surfboard under his arm.

Julia set up the meeting file to print, a smile hovering on her lips. She appreciated his diligence and determination to stay on top of his workload. So far she couldn't complain about his work ethic.

Did Sean know they'd be traveling together to Queensland in a few weeks? Had Ryan or Cassie contacted him?

Maybe Sean didn't care, but it seemed as if his presence had invaded every area of her life. Thank goodness she didn't see him at the gym. He probably preferred to surf. He was lean, fit and ate nutritious lunches. She couldn't help noticing that he looked after himself and valued his health.

Sean reappeared, showered and dressed in a T-shirt and jeans.

He headed straight for his desk, giving her a big smile. "Do you have the files ready to upload on the website?"

She nodded, handing him a USB stick. "It's in the website folder under today's date."

"Thanks." He pulled out a chair, signed on to his computer and shoved the USB in the slot.

She stared at his back, chewing her lipstick off her lower lip. "Have you spoken to Ryan lately?"

"Last night."

"Oh, did he mention the resort opening?"

"Yeah." His fingers tapped on the keyboard. "Sounds like fun."

She fidgeted with a chunky gold bracelet circling her right wrist. "Cassie gave me the flight details."

"Ryan said she'd made the bookings."

"Did you know we're traveling together?"

He nodded, his gaze remaining fixed on his computer screen. "We can share a cab to the airport."

"Hmm."

His hands paused over the keyboard. "Don't sound so excited."

"I'm looking forward to the trip. I can't wait to see Cassie again."

He swung around in his chair, his gaze piercing. "But you don't want to travel with me."

She straightened her spine, sitting taller. "I never said that."

"But it's what you're thinking. You're stuck babysitting me."

"Oh, you know about this?"

"I know my father, and he was insistent I travel with him and Mom. He was ticked when I wouldn't change my plans and go early with them."

"I see." Her conversation with Cassie now made sense.

"You know something." His voice softened. "I'd much rather travel with you than my father."

"It's only a short flight."

"Right now, ten minutes with my dad is too long."

She lifted a brow. "I hope things get better soon."

"I'm not counting on it. Dad's set in his ways. When he gets an idea in his head, it's hard to change his mind."

"He sounds like my mom."

"Is she stubborn, too?"

Julia shook her head. "It's just this whole adoption thing is unsettling her. I'm searching for my birth mom."

His eyes widened. "That's a big step."

"Mom hasn't taken the news too well. Billie has also started searching for her birth parents."

"Your mom's feeling threatened."

"I guess so. It's all getting complicated."

"Family stuff can be messy."

"Tell me about it. Are you all set to play guitar at church this weekend?"

He nodded. "I've never played with a church band before."

"You'll do great. I'll be praying for us."

"Really?"

"Yeah, when I'm singing, I pray the music will help the congregation connect with God."

"That's great. I'm a bit rusty, and I'll need all the prayers I can get."

"Everything went well at practice. It should go smoothly." Unlike her life, where nothing seemed to be going according to her plan. She seemed destined to remain single and spend more of her spare time with Sean, who didn't meet her criteria for a husband.

On Sunday evening, Julia arrived at the church half an hour early. Sean stood on the stage at the front, adjusting the settings on his guitar.

She hurried to the stage, greeted the music team and lowered the height of her microphone near Sean. "Is Matt here?"

Sean nodded. "He wants to run through all the songs now."

"No worries." She arranged her sheet music on the stand. A few people had started filing into the rows of seats. Small groups of teens gathered in the aisles, chatting among themselves in animated tones.

When Matt returned to the stage, the music team commenced their rehearsal.

Julia's throat felt better, and she hit all the right notes without any problems. She offered a silent prayer of thanks, the tension easing in her muscles.

Sean played lead guitar, his stiff stance the only indication he might be feeling a little uncomfortable.

The music practice finished a few minutes before the service was scheduled to begin. Julia followed the band members to the front row. She selected a seat next to Sean.

He leaned close and whispered, "It's weird sitting up front."

She smiled. "It's easier for us to be here. You'll get used to it."

"I'm not convinced."

She crossed her legs, her calf brushing against Sean's jeans-clad knee. A tingle of awareness shot through her, and she wriggled an extra few inches away from him.

Sean and the musicians returned to the stage, and Julia trailed behind them. She'd missed all of Simon's opening address and needed to focus on the service instead of being distracted by Sean. It seemed as if he was close by her side all the time.

She held her microphone, letting the comforting words of the opening song soothe her. The congregation joined her in worship, and she concentrated on hitting the notes in perfect pitch.

She sneaked a glance at Sean during the short break before the next song. He seemed more relaxed now. He was a talented guitarist, and she hoped he'd continue playing in the band.

She caught his eye, a smile curving up her lips.

He grinned and started playing the intro for the next song. His fingers flew over the strings and guitar neck, the tone blending with the other instruments in the band.

It sounded as though he'd been playing with them for years, not days.

The song ended and Julia returned to her seat. Simon interviewed a missionary, who had been based in Africa. The missionary described her zest and commitment to helping people in remote villages.

Hope stirred in Julia's heart. Overseas mission work was a viable option. She didn't need a husband to undertake the role, and she could indulge her enthusiasm for learning different languages.

Lord, please give me direction. I'd love to have a fulfilling career where I can help people in a practical way. I want to make a difference.

The service passed in a blur, her thoughts dwelling on the missionary's words. Before long, Julia stood behind her microphone, singing the final notes of the closing song.

At the end of the service, a group of girls in their late teens surrounded Sean. Julia overheard their gushing words. She stifled a giggle.

Sean's striking eyes implored her to extract him from the boisterous gathering of teens.

She ducked around the girls, reaching his side.

He smiled. "Can you please help me pack up?"

"Sure," Julia said.

"I'll help you," a petite brunette said, a hopeful tone in her voice.

"Thanks, but I'm okay."

"Oh." The brunette pouted, pointing to Julia. "Are you with her?"

Julia bit her lower lip, her laughter threatening to surface at any moment.

Sean cleared his throat. "Yeah, we spend a lot of time together."

"Oh." The girl's shoulders slumped forward. She signaled her friends to follow her as she walked away from Sean.

Julia laughed. "You broke her heart, you mean man."

His smile broadened. "I'm devastated. No doubt she'll find someone else to hang around."

"You do realize what you've done?"

He raised an eyebrow. "Fixed a problem?"

She shook her head. "You've created a new problem."

"How?"

"By the end of the night, everyone will think we're dating."

"You're serious?"

She nodded. "We have a very efficient church grapevine, and you said it yourself that we spend lots of time together."

"At work."

Plus church and their upcoming weekend in Queensland, but she wasn't going to mention that right now. "But you didn't say that."

"Oh. It's what I meant."

"I know."

"If I know the truth and so do you, what does it matter?"

"You really haven't spent much time around churches, have you?"

He shook his head. "I went to Sunday school when I was a kid, and quit going as soon as Mom and Dad would let me."

"Well, be prepared."

"For what?"

She chuckled. "You'll find out soon enough." Their supposed relationship would be the talk of the church for a short time, until everyone discovered they worked together and were only friends.

Julia prayed every night for her future husband. For a man who shared her enthusiasm and vision for full-time ministry. Sean didn't meet her prayer criteria. He couldn't be the man for her, despite her growing attraction. An attraction she struggled each day to ignore.

A week later, Sean completed a major upgrade of the church website. He uploaded the final version of the web pages, verifying all the new social-media links were fully operational. He also checked that the online sermon series streamed in correctly. He smiled. The audio files were clear of static and background noise.

Satisfied, he leaned back in his chair and stretched his legs. He glanced at the time on the screen, realizing it was after four. Monday afternoon had disappeared, and he'd spent the whole day absorbed in his world of coding.

Julia returned to her desk. "Time for coffee?"

"I'm done. I might take off early, if that's okay?"

"Sure. Did you skip your lunch break?"

"No. I did stop for a sandwich. I wanted to finish the last section of the website overhaul today."

She smiled. "Good work. Are you heading to the beach?"

"Maybe, depending on the conditions. Now that winter has arrived, it's too cold to stay in the water unless there's good surf to make it worthwhile."

She nodded. "The water is freezing. You won't talk me into swimming at this time of year."

"I'm borrowing a board from Ryan so I can surf when we head north to the warmer currents."

"A good idea. I might consider swimming at the beach in Queensland if it's hot enough."

He laughed. "I'll believe that when I see it. Have you completed all your work for today?"

She shook her head. "I still have a few things to finish up."

"Okay." They'd established an easygoing working relationship, and he looked forward to seeing her each day. "Do you want me to stay and help? I don't have to be anywhere."

"Nope. You deserve to leave early. I'll make a coffee. It won't take me long to get everything done."

"No worries." He stashed his gear in his backpack and shut down his computer.

The door opened and he ignored it, knowing Julia would take care of the visitors if they needed assistance. He'd learned to tune out the swishing noise that indicated someone had walked into the reception area.

A deep male voice greeted Julia.

Sean paused, his body rigid. What was his father doing here?

He spun around in his chair. His parents chatted with Julia near the door, looking at ease in her company. They weren't supposed to be in Sydney until the weekend.

Sean walked toward them, trepidation filling each step. "Hi, Mom and Dad. This is a surprise."

His mom gave him a warm hug. "How's my boy doing?"

"I'm fine." He couldn't ignore his father's icy gaze. "I wasn't expecting you to visit today."

His father frowned. "Your mother and I thought we could stay with you for a few days at Ryan's apartment before we fly to Melbourne to visit friends."

He flinched. The apartment was trashed. He'd planned to do all his laundry and a few hours of cleaning before they arrived. Too late now, unless he could distract them and go home ahead of them.

"When did you arrive?" Sean asked.

"After lunch," his mother said. "I did a little bit of cleaning for you."

His stomach sank. "You shouldn't have. I was planning to do it later, before you both arrived."

His father's frown deepened. "Your mother has spent hours cleaning this afternoon. How can you live in such a hovel?"

Julia cleared her throat. "If you'll excuse me, I have a few things to do out back." She gave Sean a sympathetic smile. "Since you're heading off soon, I'll see you tomorrow."

His father raised an eyebrow. "What time are you meant to finish?"

"Five," Sean said.

His father glanced at his wristwatch. "It's only four-thirty. Are you shirking your work responsibilities?"

"No." He clenched his fists. "Julia has printing and binding to do out back, so she's saying goodbye early."

"Is that right?" His father stared hard at Julia.

She twisted a lock of hair around her finger, holding his father's gaze. "Sean has finished his work for today. He's free to leave now if he'd like to—"

"Actually, I really should stay and help Julia," Sean

told his parents. "We don't want her working late because of me."

His mother smiled. "How considerate of you, dear." She looked at his dad. "Brian, we can wait here, can't we? I really want to spend time with our son." She patted her purse. "I brought a new novel with me to pass the time in case we had to wait."

His father scowled. "If you wish."

"That settles it," his mom said. "You two go ahead, and we'll be here when you're done."

"I need to lock the door. Is that okay?" Julia asked.

Sean's dad nodded. "I assume you have a bell outside."

"Yes, and we're not expecting any visitors." Julia secured the external door and tilted her head in Sean's direction. "Let's go."

He followed her down the hall, avoiding his father's penetrating gaze. A brief reprieve before he resumed his battle with his father after work.

Chapter 5

Julia strode into the empty meeting room behind Sean and closed the door. "What's going on?"

Sean paced the room, rubbing his hands over his face. "My parents weren't supposed to arrive until the weekend."

"Why aren't you going home now? You've done your hours, finished all your work, and your mom's waiting outside."

"I know." He paused, staring at the carpet. "If Mom was here by herself, I'd leave in a heartbeat."

She frowned. "What's up with you and your dad?"

"He's in a mood." Sean stood in front of the pile of papers on the table. "Where do you want me to start?"

"Over there." She pointed to a ream of yellow paper. "Look, you don't have to help me."

"I need a distraction." He slipped into a chair at the table. "I should have cleaned up the apartment earlier, but I thought I had more time…"

She shrugged. "It's only housework, and your mom didn't seem upset about cleaning up. Mess happens. Billie and I don't live in a spotless apartment."

"Mom likes spoiling me, but Dad is a whole different ball game." He shook his head. "I can never meet his expectations, no matter what I do or how hard I try."

"Can't he see the progress you've made, and the changes you've made to improve your life?"

He bent his head, concentrating on folding the paper in half. "He compares me to Ryan. I always come up short."

Julia pressed her lips together. She'd witnessed first-hand the struggle Sean faced to win his father's approval. At the same time, she understood why his father had issues with him over his behavior in the past. It made sense his father found it difficult to give him the benefit of the doubt.

She pulled out a chair next to him. "How can I help you?"

He raised his head, a faint smile curving his lips. "I appreciate your support."

She nodded. "Cassie and Ryan believe in you, too. Your dad will come around eventually."

"I'm not so sure. He has dug his heels in real deep this time."

"Fine, but if you keep on doing the right thing, he'll be forced to realize he's wrong about you."

"Maybe." He dropped his gaze. "The problem is it's only a matter of time until I screw up again, and he'll remind me of it forever."

She placed her hand over his for a brief moment. "I'll be praying for you."

He looked up, his eyes moist. "Thanks. I'm going need to all the prayers I can get to survive the next few days."

"You can do it, and don't forget your mom is your ally."

"She's stuck in the middle. Her support for me causes problems in her relationship with Dad."

"You're blessed to have a mother who loves you unconditionally. My mom is the same, always in my corner." If she located her birth mother, would she want to establish a relationship with her? Or did she have unrealistic expectations?

Her search for her birth mother was a risk. A big risk on an emotional level. She longed for a fairy-tale ending, but couldn't guarantee it would happen, no matter how hard she tried or how many times she prayed.

The following afternoon, Julia tidied up her workspace and reorganized the pending items in her in tray. She intended leaving work at five sharp.

Billie had plans this evening, and Julia had two hours to fill before band practice. She could go to a gym class, but she'd be pushing it to eat dinner afterward and make it back to the church on time.

Sean sauntered over to her desk, holding a mug of coffee. "You're leaving now?"

She nodded, powering off her computer. "For a change, I'm actually up-to-date and on top of everything."

"Great. Are you going to band practice?"

"Yep."

His smile widened, a dimple forming on his chin. "Why don't we grab a bite to eat beforehand?"

She tilted her head sideways, meeting his warm gaze. "I thought you'd be having dinner with your parents."

"Not tonight. I think they're going out with friends."

She grinned, trying to hide her mirth. "Oh, that works out really well for you."

"What's so funny?"

"I can tell you're glad to have an excuse to go out tonight. And I totally get why you're happy to skip dinner with your father."

He pulled his brows together. "I think the dinner arrangements were my mother's idea."

"She's a smart lady, looking out for your best interests." She lowered her tone, concern permeating her voice. "Have things improved at all with your dad?"

"Not really. Last night wasn't fun. But speaking of dinner…" He shoved his hands into his jacket pockets. "Are you in?"

She nodded. "I don't have any plans."

His eyes lit up. "What do you feel like eating?"

"I don't know. We could try out the new noodle bar that opened up opposite the beach."

"Sounds good, but I'll need at least fifteen minutes to finish up here. I'm in the middle of something, and I'll lose my train of thought if I leave it until tomorrow."

"Okay, I'll make myself a coffee. Would you like a refill?"

"No, thanks, I should be done soon."

"Sure." Smiling, she strolled down the hall to the staff room to pour herself a fresh coffee. She settled in a comfy velvet armchair in a corner of the spacious room, checking her phone messages and email while sipping her coffee.

Her face warmed, the emails on her phone failing to capture her full attention. Why had she agreed to have dinner with Sean? Tonight would be the first time since the wedding that she'd seen him in a social setting outside of work or church. She couldn't forget how their encounter at the wedding had turned out.

If only Sean hadn't been secretly drinking at the wedding. He had denied it, of course, knowing any consumption of liquor was against the rules of his rehab program. The liquor had impaired his judgment, which had led to their harsh exchange of words before he'd stormed out of the wedding reception. She questioned whether he could remember any of the details from their confrontation.

She was drawn to Sean, no doubt, and couldn't resist

spending more time with him. Would he get the wrong idea and read more into her acceptance of his casual dinner invitation? A romantic relationship with Sean wasn't an option, despite her growing admiration for him as a person.

Footsteps echoed in the hall, and Sean appeared in the doorway.

She switched off her phone. "You're finished already."

He nodded. "Let's go. I'm starved."

She gathered her belongings, locked up the office and walked down the street with him toward the noodle bar.

Sean paused in front of a surf shop, his attention glued to a top-of-the-line Jet Ski on display in the window.

"You'd like to buy one?" she asked.

"I wish, but it won't happen on my budget."

"True. Jet Skis aren't cheap." Her salary wouldn't stretch to accommodate this type of expenditure either, unless she dipped into her trust fund. She was debt-free, and had made the decision to live within her means on her current salary.

They reached the noodle bar, and Sean opened the door.

"Thanks." She entered the hip eatery ahead of him and read the menu board behind the counter.

Sean stood close beside her, his arm almost touching hers.

"What takes your fancy?" He leaned closer, his whispered words a light caress on her cheek. "Mild or spicy?"

Her pulse raced, muddling her thoughts. "I'm tossing up between pad thai and laksa."

"A tough decision."

She stepped back, putting a little more space between them. "I'll fix up my own order."

He frowned. "I can get yours with mine."

She shook her head, staring up into his vibrant eyes. "It's not as though we're on a date, and I'm more than happy to pay my way."

His eyes widened. "Yeah, right, if you insist."

"I do."

He turned away, breaking their connection. His back was to her as he studied the menu board.

Julia moved ahead in the queue, her mind whirling. Now she'd offended him and needed to make amends. "What do you feel like?"

"A large serving of one of the beef combos."

"You're just a little bit hungry?"

His eyes brightened. "I could happily live on Asian food."

"Me, too."

He grinned. "Another thing we have in common."

"Yep." Her gaze locked with his, and she couldn't remember why it might be a bad idea to have dinner with him.

Sean cupped Julia's elbow, his voice soft. "The lady is waiting for your order."

"Oh." She darted forward to the noodle bar counter, running her fingers through her windswept hair. "Um, can I please have the pad thai?"

The lady behind the counter noted her order and processed her purchase using Julia's credit card.

Julia gave Sean a hesitant smile, a wary look entering her eyes. She wasn't immune to the attraction that he couldn't deny, the magnetic pull that drew them closer against their better judgment. She'd rejected him once at the wedding, and his pride didn't need to take another hit.

Sean placed his order for satay beef and paid by cash.

He didn't own a credit card, another reminder of his broken and desperate past. His credit card abuse a few years ago had ensured no reputable company would issue him a card anytime soon.

He shoved his wallet into his jacket pocket. "Where would you like to sit? Inside or outside?"

"Indoors is fine."

They chose a table for two by the window overlooking the ocean promenade. The sunlight began to fade over the eastern horizon. The muted overhead lighting picked up the red highlights in Julia's rich, glossy hair. He settled back in his seat, opened a packet of chopsticks and poured two glasses of water.

Julia glanced at her wristwatch. "We have plenty of time before the music practice starts."

He nodded. "I'm glad you said yes to dinner."

"Me, too. We could do this again if we're both on the music roster for the same week."

He smiled. "A good idea."

Sean noticed a number of men in the restaurant sending discreet, admiring glances in Julia's direction. He was intrigued by her lack of pretension and awareness of her natural beauty. He enjoyed her company, and appreciated her genuine offer of friendship. Anything more was a bonus.

On Friday evening of the following week, Julia zipped her suitcase and wheeled it to the entrance of her apartment.

Her cell phone beeped. She read the message from Sean, letting her know the cab they were sharing to the airport would be at her place within minutes.

She walked along the front path outside her apartment complex, spotting a cab driving up her street.

After the cabbie helped her stow her suitcase in the trunk, she settled beside Sean in the backseat.

She smiled. "I can't wait to see Cassie again."

He nodded. "We should have a fun weekend."

Once they arrived at the airport, Sean settled their fare. He towed their suitcases to the short priority check-in queue inside the terminal.

She glanced at the departure board, glad to learn they had plenty of time until their flight. "What are your plans for the weekend?"

He grinned. "Surfing, of course. The beach across the road from the resort is a well-known surfing haunt. What are you planning to do?"

"I don't know. Relax, catch up with Cassie."

"You miss her."

She nodded. "We talk on the phone, but it's not the same. And she's been back to Sydney only a couple of times since the wedding."

"The process of setting up the resort and getting it running has kept her and Ryan busy."

"I know." She moved to the front of the queue. "The resort launch party tomorrow night should be fun."

He nodded. "They have good press coverage, and Ryan mentioned a few local celebrities will be there."

"I bought a new dress for the party."

His smile broadened. "I'm sure you'll look great."

Warmth enveloped her face. "Thanks. Did you bring a suit?"

He shook his head, pointing to his small suitcase. "I travel light. I'll borrow something from Ryan."

The red arrow light flashed, indicating they were next in line to check their luggage.

The lady behind the desk asked for their identification and processed their tickets. "Your seats are together, in a row at the front of the plane." She smiled. "Enjoy your weekend away."

Sean grinned. "Thanks, we will."

Julia nodded. Did the lady think they were heading off for a romantic weekend at the Sunshine Coast?

Sean cupped her elbow and guided her toward the departure gate. Their tickets gave them access to the club lounge.

She laughed. "The check-in lady seemed to think we're going away together."

He shrugged. "What does it matter?"

She frowned. "I suppose you're right." As long as they both knew the truth about their trip.

They selected a cool beverage from the bar and sat together at a table in the lounge, chatting while they waited for their boarding call.

Julia leaned back in her comfortable leather chair, crossing her legs. They were surrounded by business people in suits, couples and only a few families with kids. A group of women at a nearby table sent appreciative glances in Sean's direction.

No big surprise. He looked fabulous in his black fitted T-shirt and jeans. The women probably assumed she was Sean's girlfriend.

An unsettling thought entered her mind. What would it be like to date Sean for real? His manners were impeccable, and he had that knack for making a girl feel special. He certainly didn't lack charm or charisma.

Her heart sank. It could never happen. She knew what she wanted, and he didn't meet her criteria list.

Lord, will I ever meet a man who shares my vision for mission work? Or is this a pipe dream?

Her current work contract could end in a few months and not be renewed if her friend chose to return to work

early from maternity leave. And then what? Her trust
fund enabled her to live her dream and work full-time in
either a low-paying or volunteer job. Maybe she should
call the overseas mission organization next week and line
up an interview. It could be her best option.

Chapter 6

At noon the next day, Julia and Cassie entered the up-scale Sunshine Coast restaurant located on the third floor of the resort complex.

Ryan sat at a table for six across the room, chatting with his parents. Julia had considered declining the invitation to the family lunch, but at breakfast this morning, Sean's mother had insisted she join them.

Julia slipped into a seat beside Cassie and stared at the empty chair across the table. Where was Sean? She'd last seen him in the distance in the lobby early this morning before he had gone surfing with Ryan.

After greeting everyone, Julia placed her order with a hovering waiter and admired the tranquil ocean views through a nearby window. The restaurant had gained an excellent reputation since it had opened a few months earlier.

Sean's mother sat next to her. Julia had enjoyed talking with her during breakfast. She'd met Colleen for the first time at Cassie and Ryan's wedding. Colleen had made a big effort this weekend to help her feel welcome within the family.

Colleen smiled. "I'm glad you could make it."

Julia nodded. "Did you have a pleasant morning at the spa?"

"It was wonderful." Colleen sipped her sparkling water. "I could so easily have stayed there all day."

"Cassie and I have an appointment after lunch." Julia was treating her friend for the afternoon.

"Well, you girls have fun, and take some time out to relax."

"We will," Julia said.

The waiter arrived with their starter. Julia picked at her plate of chicken Caesar salad, moving the anchovies to one side of her plate. She'd been distracted by Sean's absence and had forgotten to order the salad without anchovies.

Sean's father crossed his arms over his chest. "Has anyone seen or heard from Sean since he went surfing this morning?"

Julia shook her head, catching Cassie's concerned gaze.

Cassie placed her fork beside her plate. "I haven't spoken to him since he checked into his room last night."

Ryan frowned. "I left him at the beach a few hours ago, and I forgot to remind him about lunch."

"I can't believe this." Sean's father clenched his fist, his fury evident in his icy tone. "What's wrong with him? Ryan, you shouldn't have to remind him that we organized a family lunch."

"Brian, calm down," Colleen said. "I'm sure Sean has a really good reason for being late."

"Stop making excuses for him. He's irresponsible, and it's about time he grew up and started behaving like an adult."

Julia dipped her head and concentrated on eating her salad. Frustration coursed through her. She hated listening to Sean's parents disagree, but she could hardly say anything in Sean's defense.

Colleen placed her hand on Brian's arm. "Let's not get

all worked up until we see Sean and find out what happened. It's possible there's a logical explanation for why he's skipped lunch."

"He's probably still surfing," Ryan said. "The surf was excellent this morning, and it's a great day to be out in the water."

Brian shook his head. "That's not a good enough excuse. I will be talking to Sean about this when I see him, and he'll be left with no illusions about my thoughts on this subject."

An hour passed, and the chair across the table remained empty.

Julia sipped her iced tea. Sean's name wasn't mentioned again, but his absence had created more tension between his parents.

When Sean's father caught up with him, Sean would have a lot of explaining to do. It wasn't going to end well.

Disappointment flooded her heart. Was Sean's father right? Could she trust Sean to keep his word, or would he ditch spending time with her if a better offer came along?

Sean wandered into the resort hotel lobby, his body invigorated from surfing in the pristine ocean. The weather was perfect, and the currents warm enough to swim in without needing a wetsuit.

He'd left his surfboard with the doorman, planning to return to his room to shower and change before heading back to the beach later in the afternoon. A couple of his old surfing buddies had been out at the break this morning, and he'd appreciated the opportunity to catch up with them. Not much had changed since he'd moved to Sydney.

His stomach rumbled. It was probably close to lunchtime, and he hadn't eaten since breakfast.

Julia lounged on a sofa in a corner of the lobby, her

attention glued to her phone. She looked relaxed in a summer dress, her bare legs crossed at the knees and a flimsy sandal dangling from one foot.

He walked over to her. "Hey, Julia."

She stood. "Where have you been?"

"Surfing. The waves were awesome."

"What about lunch?"

He frowned. "Did we arrange to meet for lunch?"

"No, I'm talking about the family lunch today that your mom kindly invited me to attend."

He closed his eyes for a second. "I totally forgot about that." He glanced around the lobby. "What's the time?"

"Nearly two."

"Really? It's that late?"

"Yep. Lunch was at twelve."

He ran his hand through his damp hair. "Dad's going to be ticked."

She nodded. "Why'd you skip lunch?"

"I didn't mean to miss lunch. The surf was up, and a couple of guys I know were out in the water. I lost track of the time."

"Is that your best excuse?"

"No, it's the truth."

"It's not me you need to convince."

"Did my dad say something?"

"He wants to talk to you."

"That figures. What are you doing now?"

She stashed her phone in her purse. "Waiting for Cassie. We have an appointment at the spa in ten minutes."

"Do you want to meet later for coffee?"

She shook her head. "Cassie and I made plans for the whole afternoon."

"Okay. I guess I'll see you tonight."

"We could walk down to the ballroom together."

"Sure." His mood lifted at the optimistic tone in her invitation. "I'll knock on your door at seven."

She smiled, her eyes brightening. "Great. I'll see you then."

He waved goodbye and headed for the bay of elevators. Tonight he wasn't going to mess up. He'd be true to his word and arrive on her doorstep at seven. And do his best to avoid spending time with his father.

Hopefully, his dad would calm down this afternoon and be in a reasonable frame of mind by this evening. Sean needed to apologize for missing the family lunch and disappointing his parents again.

A brisk knock sounded on the door to Julia's suite at seven in the evening. She finished applying her lipstick and smiled. Sean was right on time. She slipped on her new heels, grabbed her purse and swung open the door.

Sean stood on the threshold holding a single long-stemmed white rose in a delicate crystal vase.

She gasped, warmth infusing her face. "Oh, Sean, you shouldn't have. The rose is perfect."

He grinned, his eyes sparkling. "Wow, you look fabulous."

"You're looking good, too. I really like your suit." He'd made an effort with his appearance, wearing an elegant charcoal suit and sky blue silk tie.

"For you." He gave her the rose, his fingers brushing against hers.

"Thanks." A tingle flowed through her body, adding more color to her overheated face. She stepped back. "I guess I'd better find a place for this before we go."

He nodded. "A good idea."

Julia topped off the water and placed the vase on her bedside table.

Sean waited at the door. "Will you know many people at the party?"

"Only yours and Cassie's family."

"We can hang out together."

"That works for me. Do you think you'll know many people?"

"I'm not sure. I didn't live here long. Plus, I spent the majority of my time surfing, playing tennis and looking for work."

She nodded. "Cassie mentioned you're a pretty good tennis player."

"I can hold my own."

Julia closed the door to her suite and walked with Sean to the elevator. Her three-inch heels slowed her progress.

She stumbled, and he cradled her elbow while she regained her balance.

"Are you all right?" he asked.

"Yes. As you've probably guessed, my shoes are new, and I hardly ever wear heels this high." She smoothed the knee-length skirt of her forest green silk dress. "I should be fine once I get used to them."

They rode the elevator to the Grand Ballroom. At full capacity, it could seat five hundred people, and no expense had been spared during the renovation.

Sean's fingertips rested on her waist. He guided her through the throng of guests to a refreshments table at one end of the ballroom. Rows of silver platters were lined up on the long table. Numerous waiters circulated the room, distributing food and drinks to the guests.

Julia selected a sparkling water from a passing waiter. She glanced around the spacious ballroom, thankful she'd arrived with Sean. Cassie was somewhere in the crowd, mingling with her guests.

Sean sipped his soda. "Are you hungry? We could sit at one of the tables near the windows."

"A good idea."

They filled their plates with savory treats and found a vacant table for two beside a floor-to-ceiling window overlooking the ocean. A band entertained guests on the far side of the ballroom near the dance floor.

Julia let out a deep breath. "It's good to sit down."

He grinned. "I figured you'd prefer to sit since you're wearing new shoes."

"Thanks." She stared into his eyes and almost forgot where she was, entranced by the warmth emanating from them.

His voice softened. "You're welcome."

She lowered her lashes, and picked at the food on her plate. She couldn't ignore the powerful connection she'd established with Sean. It had crept up on her, building during the ever-increasing amount of time they had spent in each other's company.

Julia was flattered by his attention and the way he considered her needs. She'd gained an insight into his true character. She liked what she'd discovered. He'd made his romantic intentions clear tonight by giving her the beautiful white rose.

Sean flicked a few wavy locks of hair off his forehead and lounged back in his chair. "I haven't been to a party this posh in ages."

She nodded, recognizing a local actor walking past with her footballer boyfriend. "Cassie and Ryan should get great exposure for the resort."

"Yeah, I saw at least half a dozen photographers following the A-list crowd. Have you seen Cassie or Ryan tonight?"

She shook her head. "I imagine they're busy mingling with their guests. Cassie did mention that a number of golfing pros would be here, too."

"Makes sense. They're building a first-class golf course behind the tennis courts out back."

"Did you catch up with your dad this afternoon?"

"Nope." He dropped his gaze and nibbled on a chicken-satay stick.

"You'll probably see him tonight."

He shrugged his shoulders. "Maybe, although with a crowd this big, we may not run into him or my mom."

She sipped her drink. "You'll have to talk with him sooner or later. I got the feeling he's not going to forget what happened today for a long time."

"I'd rather talk about you than worry about my old man." His smile widened. "I like what you've done with your hair. Very sophisticated."

Her heart warmed at his genuine compliment. "The hairdresser at the spa thought it would work well with my dress." She ran her fingers over the elaborate arrangement of curls above the nape of her neck.

"You look just as stunning as the celebrities wandering around here, if not better," he said.

"I don't think so."

"No, seriously. You keep yourself in great shape, and I've noticed a number of admiring glances flying your way."

"At the end of the day, it's who you are on the inside that matters, not the outside package."

"Yeah, I kind of learned that lesson the hard way."

He piqued her curiosity. "Why? What happened?"

"It's a long story I'd rather forget. Do you like olives?"

She nodded. "The stuffed green olives are my favorite."

He spiked an olive with a toothpick and leaned toward her, but then he groaned. "My parents are heading our way."

She turned her head and waved at Sean's mom. His dad's mouth was a thin straight line.

Julia greeted Sean's parents, appreciating their genuine and warm welcome.

Sean smiled. "Hey, Mom, Dad."

"Where have you been?" his father asked. "I've been looking for you all afternoon, and you've ignored my messages."

"Around," Sean said. "I was busy doing stuff this afternoon. It's a great party, isn't it?"

Brian's eyes narrowed. "Don't change the subject. Where were you at lunch?"

Sean sipped his drink. "Surfing. Sorry about lunch. I was planning to be there, but lost track of the time."

"How convenient," Brian said.

"It's the truth." Sean drained his glass. "Julia, would you like a refill?"

Her stomach tightened into a hard knot. "I'm fine, thanks." She couldn't ignore the tension charging the air, the anger emanating from Sean's father.

Brian looked Julia straight in the eye, his eyes firm and unyielding. "Cassie's over by the band. Why don't you go and find her? I'm sure she can introduce you to a few of her friends."

She gulped, taken aback by his words. "Well, actually, I'm okay here with Sean."

Brian glared at his son. "Stop wasting Julia's time. You know she's too good for someone like you."

Sean recoiled as if he'd been slapped in the face. "What did you say?"

"You heard me right. Julia deserves someone better than you."

"But we're not in a relationship," Julia said. "We're friends, work colleagues. I'm his supervisor."

Brian frowned. "It didn't look that way to me."

Chapter 7

Sean stood, thrusting his hands on his hips. "Dad, you have no right to tell Julia what to do. She's not your daughter."

Brian squared his shoulders. "But you're my son, and I know what you're like."

"Brian." Colleen took hold of his arm. "This is ridiculous. It's time for us to leave. You can talk to Sean later, when you've calmed down."

Brian ignored his wife, shaking off her hand and pulling out a chair beside Julia. "Don't let my son fool you. He can be very charming when he feels like it."

Sean fumed, his frustration with his father gaining momentum.

"You have nothing to worry about," Julia said. "I can take care of myself. Sean has changed, and he's now a better person than before."

"You're a nice girl," Brian said. "I'd hate to see my son hurt you."

This was unbelievable. "Dad, just drop it, okay. We're not little kids."

Brian stood, his mouth set in an obstinate line. "I'll believe that when you start acting like a responsible adult."

Sean bit his lip, determined to stay quiet and not utter words in anger that he'd later regret.

His mom pulled him into a brief, loving hug. "We can talk about this some other time."

"Thanks, Mom." Sean braced his body, preparing for more verbal hits from his father. Anger flowed through him, and his eyes searched Julia's.

She stood, frown lines forming between her brows. "I think I should leave so you can all work this out."

"No," Sean said. "I'm outta here, too." He grabbed hold of Julia's hand, leading her away from his parents.

Her soft fingers tensed in his tight grip.

"What's going on?" she asked.

He slowed his pace, letting go of her hand. "This is normal."

"Really?"

He nodded. "Dad's had this attitude with me ever since I accidentally drove his truck into a creek."

"You what?" She walked beside him, weaving around the groups of people gathered in the ballroom. "Sean, please tell me you're joking."

"It was years ago, when I was eighteen, and not long before Dad sold the farm." Sean had been young and stupid. He had lost control of the truck late one night on the back road near the farm. After struggling to wade out of the creek, he'd walked home and collapsed in bed. The next morning, he'd woken to find his father standing over his bed, yelling at him about the damage to the truck.

"What happened?" She met his gaze, her eyes wide. "You obviously didn't drown with the truck."

He chuckled. "It's a bit difficult to drown in three feet of water. Look, it's a long story I'd rather forget."

She wrinkled her nose. "I suppose Ryan didn't do anything that big to upset your father."

He shook his head. "Ryan never did anything wrong as far as our father was concerned."

"I imagine it isn't easy to live in Ryan's shadow."

"Yep." He paused outside the ballroom, his stress levels starting to decrease. "What do you want to do now?"

"I don't know, but your mom has followed us."

His mom rushed through the ballroom entrance, coming to a halt a few feet in front of them.

She placed her hand on Julia's forearm. "I'm so sorry. I don't know what got into Brian to give you a lecture."

"It's okay," Julia said. "I know he has good intentions."

Sean gritted his teeth. "I think you're being too generous."

"Now, Sean," his mother said, a terse tone in her voice. "You've got to stop provoking your father. We hardly see you these days, and I was so disappointed you missed our family lunch."

Remorse over his carelessness subdued his anger. "Mom, I'm sorry." He hugged her. "I never meant to upset you."

His mom frowned. "Your father's right. You do need to take your responsibilities and commitments more seriously. If you say you're going to be somewhere, you need to keep your word and make sure you don't get sidetracked."

"Okay, I'll make an effort just for you."

Julia coughed. "Stop patronizing your mother. You know what she's saying is the truth, and makes sense."

He closed his eyes for a moment. Julia's perceptive take of the situation was spot-on. "All right, Mom. I'll try. But it's hard to do this when Dad's been holding a grudge for years."

His mom pursed her lips. "And you haven't?"

Her quietly spoken question spiked him with little pinpricks of guilt. "It takes two to compromise and reach some sort of truce."

"I'll keep working on your father. But you need to keep your side of the bargain."

He stared at his shoes. He'd need to make a much bigger effort to mend his ways in his father's eyes.

"The deal sounds fair," Julia said.

He read the tender compassion in her eyes. Julia was on his side. She wanted to believe he'd become a better person.

"Okay, Mom. I'll give it a go."

"Thank you." His mother smiled. "Please join us for breakfast tomorrow morning before your father and I leave for the airport."

He sucked in a deep breath, praying he'd have the strength to handle his father in a civil manner. "Can you please call my room half an hour beforehand? That way I'll have time to get ready?"

"Absolutely." His mother took hold of both his hands. "I believe in you. Your father will come around."

"I hope so."

"I better get back to him and check he hasn't burst a blood vessel in my absence."

"Okay, Mom. Thanks for listening."

"You're welcome." His mom hurried back into the ballroom.

He turned to Julia. "I need a coffee."

She nodded. "We could go to the café downstairs."

"That works for me."

Sean exhaled. He was thankful he had time to calm down before he had to see his father at breakfast tomorrow.

Julia stirred a packet of sugar into her hot chocolate, seeking a sugar hit after the drama in the ballroom. She glanced over Sean's shoulder. The busy café had only a few spare tables. Saturday night appeared to be a busy night. She was overdressed compared to the casual holidaymaker and surfer crowd.

Sean loosened his tie. "Thanks for leaving the ballroom with me."

"No problem." She wiggled her toes, which were confined by the straps of her sandals. "I really should have worn these shoes in before tonight."

"Blisters?"

She nodded. "They're not too bad, and it helps to sit down." A break from the tension in the ballroom was a welcome relief. Sean's dad had a short fuse, like his son.

Brian's words taunted her. Deep down, did she think she was better than Sean because of his shady past? Even though he'd turned his back on his old life and started over?

Sean may not fulfill her potential-husband criteria list, but her growing feelings for him weren't listening to logic or reason.

He smiled, and her heart skittered to an irregular beat. All dressed up, he looked way too attractive for her own good.

She dunked a marshmallow into her hot chocolate, swirling the gooey pink mixture into the chocolate milk. Somehow she needed to rein in her unruly thoughts and ignore the way her pulse raced into overdrive when she was near him.

Her phone beeped and she searched for it in her purse, glad for the distraction. She checked the screen. Cassie. She wanted to speak with her ASAP. No doubt her friend had talked with Sean's parents.

He raised an eyebrow. "Anyone important?"

"Cassie. If you'll excuse me, I need to use the restroom and also return her call."

"No worries. I'm not going anywhere."

"Thanks, I'll be back soon." Julia left the table and dialed Cassie's cell phone. It was better to have this conversation out of Sean's earshot. He'd started to calm down, and she didn't want him to get all riled up again.

Sean watched Julia as she headed for the restrooms. She looked sensational tonight, and he'd hardly been able to keep his eyes off her. If only he'd managed to avoid running into his father. His dad had a habit of ruining every good thing that happened in his life.

Minutes later, Julia slipped back into her seat opposite him.

"Is everything okay?" he asked.

She nodded. "I told Cassie we'd be back at the party soon."

"Did she say much?"

"Not really. Your mom told her what happened with your dad, and she just wanted to check you're okay."

Sean sipped his coffee and frowned. "I still can't believe my dad said those things to you."

"It's okay."

He clenched his fist. "No, it's not." His father was too perceptive by half. He had guessed Sean's intentions with Julia. How dare his father try to dictate whom he dated? His personal life was none of his father's business.

Julia arched an eyebrow. "At least your father cares about you. I have no idea who my birth parents are, if they're still alive or if my birth mother has actually consented to making contact."

He let out a long breath and rubbed his hand along his jaw. "I know I should be more grateful but, to be blatantly honest, Dad drives me crazy."

A smile played at the corners of her mouth. "I kind of got that impression tonight."

"Yeah, well, subtlety isn't my strong suit." He leaned forward. "Have you received any information regarding the status of your application?"

She shook her head. "I called the customer service number last week, and they said I should receive a letter soon."

"I hope it contains good news."

"Me, too, and I'm praying Billie also receives her letter soon." She stirred her drink, swirling the marshmallow froth in her mug. "My sister's now driving me crazy by obsessing over the whole thing. She hates waiting. I try not to think about it too much."

"I imagine it's scary, not knowing who or where your mom is, or if she even wants to know you."

Julia sipped her hot chocolate. "All I can do is trust that God has a plan, and remember that He'll look after me whatever happens."

He nodded. "I'm not real good at the trust thing."

"I struggle, too, especially with this issue." She sighed. "Sometimes I wish I'd left well enough alone and not started searching for her."

Her lip trembled, and he wanted to reach out and comfort her, protect her. Instead, he kept his hands on his coffee mug and stared into her gorgeous eyes. "It's probably better to learn the truth rather than living your life wondering what would have happened if you'd tried to find her."

"I guess you're right, but I can't help worrying about it. What if she's an awful person?"

He laughed. "Not likely, since she gave birth to you. I'm sure it will all work out okay."

"I hope so. Otherwise I've wasted a whole lot of

time that I could have spent doing something more constructive."

"Such as?"

"I don't know." She inspected her fingernails. "I could prepare for my next job interview."

He raised an eyebrow. "You still have a few months until your contract at the church ends." He'd miss her when the permanent receptionist returned from maternity leave.

"If I want to do overseas mission work, I'll have months of preparation work to organize, plus training."

His jaw dropped. "You're looking to move overseas?"

"Well, it's my plan B."

Trepidation filled his mind. "And what's plan A?"

She groaned. "If I tell you, you're going to laugh at me."

"No, I won't."

"Promise?"

"Yep, so spill it."

"I had hoped to marry a pastor so I could have a family and also work in a ministry role."

His mouth opened, but no words came out.

"You seem surprised," she said. "I thought you'd find the whole idea utterly ridiculous."

He shook his head. "I think you'd make a great pastor's wife."

"Maybe, but I have one big problem. I haven't met a suitable candidate."

He bit his lip, refusing to let her see he was elated that she hadn't met her ideal man. The full impact of her revelation hit him square in the jaw. How could he compete with her ideas concerning her perfect future husband? He could never measure up to such high expectations.

His stomach sank. Maybe his father was right, and she

was way out of his league. He cleared his throat. "Do you mind if I ask why?"

"What do you mean?"

"Why do you have your heart set on marrying a pastor? You've got to admit it's an unusual goal."

"Well, I guess it's hard to explain." She fiddled with a curl that had fallen loose behind her ear. "For quite a while, before I took my current job, I've felt compelled to consider doing some kind of Christian work full-time. Marrying a pastor sort of seemed logical, if that makes sense."

He narrowed his eyes, not following the logic of her argument. "So becoming a missionary is the next best thing."

"Maybe. I'm a little hazy on the details, but I know in my heart I want to spend my life helping people."

He nodded. "An admirable goal."

She lifted a brow. "You're looking at me strangely."

He drew in a steadying breath. "You've got to admit, it's an unusual career goal. I'm new to the whole church thing, and only just learning about this stuff."

She straightened in her seat. "I need to keep praying. Finding my birth mom could change my plans, too. I might not want to live overseas if I'm trying to establish a relationship with her."

"I hear you." He drank the remains of his coffee. His anger with his father had cooled to a low simmer.

Julia's future plans now filled his mind, distracting him from his troubles with his father. Was it possible he could fit into her plans? Or should he accept that friendship was all he could hope to share with her?

He glanced at his watch. "We probably should get back to the party before Cassie comes looking for us."

"You're right." She finished her drink. "She won't be happy if we don't hurry up and see her soon."

They stood, and he escorted Julia back to the party. If only their time alone together could last longer.

Chapter 8

The next morning, Julia exited the elevator and met Sean in the resort lobby. She'd indulged in a lazy start to the day, a sleep-in followed by room service for breakfast. Cassie had stopped by her suite earlier before racing off to her brunch date with Ryan and her family.

Sean smiled. "Are you ready?"

"I guess so. How did breakfast go with your parents?"

He shrugged. "It was okay. I arrived early, which made my dad happy."

"That's good. When are you going to tell me about your surprise?" Last night, they'd arranged to see each other after breakfast. Sean had sent her a message earlier this morning, asking if she could meet him in the lobby at nine-thirty.

"When we're outside," he said.

He headed for the main entrance, and she fell into step beside him.

"Why the big secret?"

"I didn't want you to chicken out."

"Oh." She paused at the exit, greeting the concierge before returning her attention to Sean. "Do you think I'm boring?"

He laughed. "Of course not." He pointed to a Harley-Davidson road bike parked outside on the drive. "What do you think?"

"Nice bike." The polished chrome glinted in the morning sun. Someone had kept the bike in top shape.

His smile widened as they strolled toward it. "Have you ridden a Harley before?"

"Nope." She tilted her head to the side. "You underestimate me."

He raised an eyebrow. "Is that so?"

She grinned. "I happen to like motorbikes."

"Great. I've planned a trip to Noosa and the hinterland this morning, if you're interested."

"That sounds like fun." She ran her finger along the seat. "I hope you have a license."

He nodded. "I wouldn't risk Ryan's new toy."

"That's good to know."

He placed a helmet in her hands. "This should fit okay."

She secured the helmet on her head, and then straddled the seat behind him.

"Hang on." He revved the powerful engine.

She circled her arms around his waist, thankful he'd suggested she wear jeans and her sensible low-heeled leather boots.

Her hair whipped behind her as they rode along the beach road. She held on tight, leaning her body into Sean's muscular back. The tangy sea breeze invigorated her senses and she relaxed, enjoying the ride with Sean.

A short while later, they reached Hastings Street in Noosa. They stopped for coffee at a café overlooking the sundrenched beach before heading west into the hinterland.

The fresh mountain air cooled her face. They climbed higher along a winding road, passing through a few small towns.

Sean parked the bike next to a quaint stone church. A number of people were filtering into the historic building.

Julia glanced at the sign outside the church. "It looks as though their morning service starts soon."

"Would you like to join them?"

"Why not?" She liked attending Sunday services when she was away from home, and she'd considered going to church with Cassie and Ryan this evening.

She removed her helmet and ran her fingers through her hair, untangling a couple of knots. An older lady greeted them with a friendly smile on the church steps, and Julia followed Sean into an empty pew at the rear of the church.

The peaceful atmosphere flowed over her, and she admired the sun-filled stained glass windows.

A middle-aged pastor led the opening address, and before Julia knew it, the traditional one-hour service was drawing to a close. She'd appreciated the pastor's dry humor during his insightful sermon from the Psalms.

Julia stood with Sean for the closing song, flicking through the hymnbook as the organist played the opening chords of "Amazing Grace."

She turned to Sean. The words of the old hymn filled her mind. For weeks, she'd been rehearsing their rendition of the hymn for the upcoming charity concert.

She sang the words and looked at him. His deep voice washed over her, and a surreal contentment filled her heart. There was something right about today, as if they were meant to be standing in this church, singing this hymn together.

The song ended, and Sean brushed a lock of hair off her face.

She remained still, his fingertips trailing a delicate path over the contours of her flushed cheekbone.

"You've memorized all the words," he said.

She nodded. "We need to practice together soon."

"I'm looking forward to it." He dropped his hand, a soft smile on his lips. "I guess we should join the queue for the door."

She shuffled along the pew ahead of him, disturbing new thoughts floating in her mind. Her connection with Sean had grown stronger this weekend. She had prayed for clarity, knowing she had big career decisions to finalize before her current work contract ended.

Where did Sean fit into her future? And why did it now feel so right to have him by her side?

The next day, Sean followed Julia to their side of the tennis court. Ryan and Cassie wandered over to the other side of the net. After a light lunch in the resort restaurant, they'd decided to play a game of mixed doubles with his brother and sister-in-law before their flight back to Sydney that night.

Julia jogged beside him to the baseline.

She smiled. "We have an excellent chance of winning, if you're as good a player as Cassie has said."

"We'll see. Ryan's weakness is his backhand, although he's very agile at the net and will volley well."

Julia nodded. "Okay. Cassie's not so good at the net. We can always try to draw her in instead of Ryan."

"Sounds like a plan." He retrieved two tennis balls from near the fence and started their warm-up.

Julia hit a beautiful forehand, and appeared at home on the court. She smashed a winner into the corner, and he realized they had a great chance of beating Ryan and Cassie. An unusual occurrence for him to do anything better than his big brother. Here was his opportunity to shine and impress Julia at the same time.

Sean served two aces in his opening game. Julia sent him a dazzling smile when they wrapped up the game without losing a point. Ryan's service game proved a tougher proposition and, after a number of deuce points, his brother stole the game away.

Julia jogged to Sean's side of the court during the change of service. "I'll work on mixing up my service game."

He nodded. "I'll be ready."

She served strong and fast, and he wondered if she'd played competitive tennis in her youth. His instincts kicked in, and he learned to anticipate Julia's game. She picked the holes in their opponent's game and wasn't afraid to exploit any opportunities that were thrown her way.

He volleyed the winning point, securing her service game.

Julia crossed to his side of the court, her hand raised for a victorious high five.

He grinned. "We're doing well."

"I know. We need to maintain our focus. Cassie has a slower second serve, which we can nail down the line."

"Do you ever stop thinking strategy and just have fun?"

She laughed. "Strategy is fun. My high school coach used to say I took everything too seriously."

"Did you play junior representative tennis?"

She nodded. "I made it as far as the regional level in the school comps, but I didn't have the ambition or drive to push any higher." She checked the tension in her racquet strings. "There were more interesting things to do than spend hours training on the court or in the gym."

"You do know how to chill and play for fun, though?"

"Of course, but this game has a lot riding on it. I've never beaten Ryan and Cassie in mixed doubles. Today is a great opportunity to remedy this situation. The victory will be sweet."

"Now I'm really feeling the performance pressure."

She laughed and moved into position on the backhand court. Cassie was at the baseline, ready to serve.

They won the first set in a tiebreak, and he jogged with Julia to the gazebo beside the court. Cassie had organized refreshments for their short break.

Cassie smiled. "Now, Julia, don't rub it in."

"If you say so." She sipped her bottled water. "I'll remember this day for a very long time."

Ryan shook his head. "Sean, your game has really improved since the last time we played."

He nodded. "I've been working on my fitness. My early-morning run is reaping rewards."

Julia raised her eyebrows. "Do you run every morning?"

"Most mornings. Sometimes I only jog to the beach and back with my board."

"I'm impressed."

"Me, too," Cassie said. "My fitness has gone downhill since we moved here. Too much work to do…"

Ryan munched on a crisp red apple. "The initial work to open the resort is done, and we can have a life again soon."

"When are you planning to visit us in Sydney?" Julia asked.

"We're not sure yet," Cassie said. "I need to meet with Dad soon to go over the next stage of the resort redevelopment. He's so hard to catch these days, and he was here only for one night to attend the official opening."

Ryan smiled. "We'll set up the meeting in Sydney and try to combine it with a holiday."

"Sounds great," Julia said.

Sean drained his bottle of chilled water, his dry throat refreshed. "Are we all ready for round two?"

Julia leaped to her feet. "Absolutely." She walked back on the court with Sean. "I have a question for you."

"Shoot." He stood at the baseline, checking the string tension in his racquet.

"We have an interchurch social tennis group that plays on Saturday afternoons. A few times each year, we play a round-robin competition day." She paused, her gaze hopeful. "We have a comp day coming up next month, and I was wondering if you'd like to be my partner?"

He gave her a big smile. "Sure. It sounds fun."

"We'd have an excellent chance of winning."

"What's the prize?"

Her eyes shimmered in the afternoon sunlight. "Dinner at a local Italian restaurant owned by the family of one of our players. We all throw in money to cover the court hire, a barbecue lunch and the dinner prize."

"We'd better start practicing soon to ensure we're playing in sync by the time the tournament starts."

She nodded. "Are you free on Saturday afternoons? We could always do with a few extra players, and we could practice our game together."

"What time?"

"Around two. We have a three-hour booking."

"That shouldn't be a problem."

She smiled. "Thank you."

"It's no biggie." He glanced across the court. Ryan and Cassie were waiting for them to get into position. "We'd better get moving."

She looked over her shoulder. "Yeah, we have another set to win."

He chuckled before jogging to the net. New ambition inspired him to play well. He'd pull out all stops to win the competition, and the opportunity to take Julia out to a nice restaurant for dinner.

His budget didn't stretch far enough to afford expensive dinners for two. Tomorrow, he'd ramp up his fitness regime and start training for the competition. For some reason, it was important for Julia to win, and he wanted to make her happy. And share a potentially romantic dinner with her. A big incentive he couldn't turn down.

Julia finished drying her hair and heard Cassie's distinctive knock on her suite door. She'd showered and changed after her energetic and exciting mixed doubles match win with Sean. A grueling second set had turned into a tightly fought battle until Sean had hit the winning point.

She let Cassie into her suite, her mouth curved into a big smile.

Cassie lifted a brow. "You look like the cat who got the cream."

"Yep." She gathered up the clothes on her bed and folded them into her suitcase. "It had to happen one day. You and Ryan aren't invincible."

Cassie laughed. "Sean's been working on his fitness. I don't remember him moving that fast around the court a few months ago."

"I'm not complaining. He's agreed to be my partner in the church tennis comp next month."

"Oh, I get it. You want to show what's-his-name that he made a mistake in dumping you."

"Cassie, I'm not that calculating." A cheeky smile played on her lips. "Liam and his new girlfriend think they're unbeatable, and I might derive a small amount of pleasure in proving them wrong."

Cassie wrinkled her nose. "And show Liam he made a mistake. Surely you don't want him back?"

She shook her head. "No way, I just want to even the score."

"And use my good-looking brother-in-law to help your cause."

"It's not like that." She zipped up her case and wandered around the suite, checking she'd packed everything for her flight home in a few hours. "I really like playing tennis with Sean."

"I know." Cassie grinned. "Ryan and I both know this."

"Huh." She nibbled on her lower lip. "What's the big deal?"

"I'm not blind. I can see how much you two like each other. It's as if you both have flashing neon signs on your foreheads."

Julia paused beside her bed. "He's a nice guy, but there's nothing's going on. We're friends, that's all."

Cassie laughed. "You could have fooled me. You really can't expect me to believe that after what's happened this weekend."

"But it's true. We're friends, nothing more." They were closer friends than they'd been at the start of the weekend, but that was okay. They'd shared a fun and enjoyable long weekend together.

"You two have been inseparable for the past few days. Sean's falling for you big time and, if you were honest with yourself, you'd admit you have similar feelings for him."

"I think you're reading a little too much into all this."

Cassie narrowed her eyes. "Be careful with him. He's making good progress in rebuilding his life, and I'd hate to see him regress."

"I've no intention of hurting Sean. You have nothing to worry about."

"Maybe. Is the prize for winning the tennis comp still dinner at that expensive Italian restaurant?"

She nodded, thankful Cassie had changed the subject. In recent months, her friend had taken on the role of Sean's overprotective sister.

Cassie crossed her arms over her chest.

"But, Cassie, I came so close to winning last time." She'd partnered with Liam, her new nemesis, a few months before they'd dated. They'd lost the final match by the smallest of margins.

"I think you have an excellent chance of winning, and Sean will be very motivated to win."

"You think so? He seems more laid-back than competitive."

Cassie let out a sigh. "He'll be motivated by the prize. You must realize this is significant."

"It's a nice restaurant."

"And a great location for a romantic dinner."

Julia lifted a brow. Her focus on beating Liam had distracted her from considering this possibility. "Well, we have to win first."

"My guess is Sean will start training tomorrow."

She hoped so. Friends went out for dinner together all the time, and Sean was great company. It was no big deal. With any luck they could celebrate their victory in style and enjoy a delicious meal together.

Chapter 9

A week later, Julia sipped her morning latte at her reception desk. She checked the time on her computer screen. Ten past nine, and no sign of Sean.

She nibbled her lower lip. He'd made a habit of being punctual, often starting work before nine. Had something gone wrong?

The phone rang and she picked up the handset, delivering her usual greeting.

"Julia, it's Sean."

"Hey, where are you?"

"At home. My Jeep won't start." His annoyance radiated through the phone line.

She frowned. He needed to update it to a newer model. His Jeep was probably older than she. "Have you called for roadside service?"

"Not yet. The wait can be long, and I thought it would be better if I walked to work now and sorted this out tonight."

"Sure, if that's what you want to do."

"I'll be there ASAP, and I'll catch up the time later in the week."

"Okay. I hope the problem with your Jeep is an easy fix."

"Me, too. I'd better get moving."

"See you soon." She ended the call and clicked open

her email program. They had a light workload today, typical for a Tuesday, and a staff meeting scheduled for eleven. She had nothing urgent in her in tray. Sean may be looking for extra work to do by the end of the day.

Sean arrived at the office half an hour later, carrying a box of donuts.

She smiled. "You didn't have to bring treats."

He handed her the box, and then tossed his backpack underneath his desk. "Have you forgotten it's my turn to buy something for our staff meeting?"

She peeked inside, inhaling the comforting bakery aroma. "Oh, you chose my favorites. Thank you."

"You're welcome. I've learned all about yours and Simon's weakness for chocolate-iced donuts."

"Yep. Anything chocolate works for us." Hunger pangs assaulted her belly, even though she'd only eaten breakfast a few hours earlier. "I can drop you home after work to save you from having to trek up the hill."

His smile widened. "Great. Why don't we pick up pizzas for dinner? You can keep me company while I wait for the roadside service, and we can practice our song for the concert."

"Do I get to choose the pizza?"

"As long as there are no olives on it."

"I can manage that." She'd phone her favorite gourmet pizza restaurant later today and place their order.

He collected the donut box from her desk. "I'll take them out back now so we'll have enough donuts for the meeting."

"A good plan. They're very tempting."

He winked and strode down the hall with the box.

She leaned back in her seat, appreciating his thoughtfulness. Curiosity about Sean's apartment filled her mind. Was his apartment as messy as his father had implied?

They needed to practice for the concert soon, since their performance was only a few weeks away. She'd stay at his place for an hour or so before heading home. Hopefully, the roadside service would be able to fix his Jeep.

After work, Julia drove her Honda into a visitor parking space outside Sean's apartment complex. She collected the bags of food from the back and followed Sean into the foyer.

He juggled the pizza boxes in one hand and inserted his security key in the elevator lock.

She giggled. "Can I hold the pizzas for you? You're about to drop them and ruin our dinner."

He shook his head, balancing the edge of the boxes against the wall. "I'm okay, and you already have your hands full with salad and garlic bread."

"True." The door opened, and she stepped into the empty elevator. The tantalizing aroma of pizza and garlic bread filled the elevator.

Minutes later, she entered Sean's apartment, and admired the incredible views of the harbor and Manly Wharf. "The view is awesome. You can see the roof of my apartment building in the distance."

He plunked the pizza boxes on the center island in the immaculate kitchen. "Really, which one?"

"The red roof next to the sandy brick tower on the waterfront. It overlooks Fairlight Beach and the rock pool."

He joined her by the window. "Yeah, I see it in the distance. That makes us nearly neighbors."

She laughed. "If I waved at you across the harbor from my roof." She placed the bags of food on the dining table. "When's the roadside service due?"

"Not for at least thirty minutes. We have time to eat first."

"Good." She set the table, and then found a bottle of chilled water in the fridge. Sean ate healthy food at home as well as work, judging by the lack of prepackaged junk food in his fridge and pantry.

Sean grabbed two dinner plates and water glasses from a cupboard. He sat beside Julia at the dining table.

Their seats faced the window, providing a clear view of the harbor, Manly Wharf and surrounding waterfront suburbs.

"May I say grace?" he asked.

"Sure." She closed her eyes, grateful he wanted to bless their food. His faith had grown and matured during the short time he'd worked at their church.

"Lord, thank You for this food and great company. I pray they can fix my Jeep today. Amen."

"Amen." She smiled, touched by his simple and heartfelt prayer.

"Let's dig in," he said.

She sampled a slice of melt-in-your-mouth vegetarian pizza, without the olives. "Delicious, as usual."

He nodded. "The seafood combo is good, too."

She picked at her green salad, her gaze roaming around the spacious and tidy apartment. Ryan had left it furnished, no doubt planning to stay here when he and Cassie visited Sydney.

An acoustic guitar was propped up beside a sofa near the window. "You have your guitar out and ready for our practice?"

He nodded. "It lives beside the sofa. I play my guitar in the evening, sometimes while watching the sun set."

Vivid hues of pink and orange lit up the western sky outside the panoramic windows. She could curl up on the sofa facing the windows and listen to him strum his guitar.

She pressed her lips together. What was she thinking, letting romantic thoughts fill her mind? They were friends sharing dinner, that was all. After they practiced their song, she'd go home and try to forget about his lazy smile and mesmerizing eyes.

After Sean finished clearing the dinner dishes, he stashed the leftover pizza in the fridge. The coffee machine was plugged in on the counter, ready for action after he sorted out the fiasco with his broken Jeep downstairs.

The doorbell buzzed. He answered the call and arranged to meet the mechanic in the parking garage.

Julia stood at the kitchen sink, rinsing their dinner plates. "Was that your roadside service?"

He nodded. "Do you want to stay here or come downstairs with me?"

She opened the dishwasher. "I can finish packing the dishwasher and cleaning up—"

"No, I'll tidy later. You don't need to clean up after me." His father had done enough of that, and complained about it the whole time, during his last visit.

Sean suspected his parents' frequent visits before his trip to Queensland were their way of checking up on him. He had been relieved when they'd cancelled a planned trip to Sydney to see him this week.

Julia slid a plate into the dishwasher. "I'll follow you downstairs."

They made their way to the parking garage. He let the mechanic in through the security gate. Sean popped open the Jeep's hood, exposing the engine to the bright fluorescent lighting.

Within minutes the mechanic raised his head, his expression grim. "Can you turn over the engine?"

"No problem." Sean put the Jeep in Neutral and turned the key.

He groaned. The noisy engine didn't sound normal. He switched off the motor and stepped out of the Jeep.

The mechanic rubbed his forehead. "You need a new fan belt, and probably an alternator, too."

Sean's stomach lurched. "Okay." How much was a new fan belt and alternator going to cost? He barely had enough money to buy food until his fortnightly salary arrived in his bank account next week.

"The engine's not sounding too flash, either. When was the last time you had it serviced?"

He frowned. "I only bought the Jeep a few months ago, and I know it's due for a service."

"We don't carry the parts you need, but I'll give you the specs." The mechanic pulled out a notepad from his pocket. "You can buy them from an auto shop and your mechanic can fit it, or we can do it for a small fee."

The man handed him a piece of paper.

Sean cringed, the price estimate unaffordable on his current budget. "Is this the cheapest way to fix it?"

The mechanic nodded. "Has the Jeep been losing power?"

"Yeah, and making that screeching noise."

"I recommend you don't drive it until you replace the parts, otherwise you could end up stranded somewhere when the belt fully breaks apart or the alternator stops working."

"Thanks for your help," Sean said.

"No worries." The mechanic lowered the hood, packed up his gear and left the parking garage.

Julia frowned. "What are you going to do?"

He shrugged, his mind spinning in a few different directions. "I'll get it fixed sometime."

"Let me know if you need a lift to the auto shop tomorrow."

He locked up the Jeep and walked with her to the elevator. "I'm not sure if I'll have time tomorrow."

She tilted her head. "I thought you'd want to get your Jeep back on the road as soon as possible."

He ran his hand through his hair. "I'll get it sorted sometime over the next few weeks."

"Are you sure?"

"Yeah, I'll add it to my list of things to do. I can live without wheels, walk to work. No big deal."

The elevator door opened and he stepped inside, swiped his card and selected his floor.

"You know," Julia said, "I'm more than happy to help you get your Jeep fixed sooner rather than later."

He smiled, appreciating the concern in her voice. "Thanks, I'll keep you posted."

"Okay."

The elevator arrived on his floor, and they stepped out. "I have a few expenses coming up."

"Tell me about it. The bills seem to turn up all at once."

"True. I do have an old friend who can probably cut me a good deal for the service and repairs."

"That's helpful."

He opened his apartment door and motioned for her to enter first.

She dashed straight for the kitchen. "Is it coffee time?"

"Definitely." He searched the pantry, finding a selection of coffee pods that worked with the machine. "Which flavor would you like?"

She scrutinized the boxes, her brows drawn together. "The Belgium chocolate mocha looks good."

"No problem." He collected two mugs from the cupboard, and then set up the machine to make her mocha.

The sky had darkened outside. The building and street-lights across the harbor glowed like stars in an inky night sky. Clouds hid the moon from view, and a lone ferry cruised toward Manly Wharf.

Julia leaned back against the kitchen counter. "This smells good."

He passed her a steaming mug, milky froth sprinkled with chocolate topping the creamy liquid.

"Thanks." She stirred in the froth, inhaling the strong aroma of coffee mingled with chocolate.

He set to work making a cappuccino for himself. "There are cookies in the container on the counter."

"I'm fine, thanks." She sipped her drink. "This is good. I'll grab a glass of water later, for when I'm singing."

"You need to look after your voice."

"It's harder in winter, but I try."

"It's getting cooler in the mornings."

Her lips curved into a smile. "You'll adjust soon, after the hardship of living in sunny Queensland with warm weather all year round."

He shook a light layer of powdered chocolate on top of his cappuccino. "It does sometimes get chilly in the mornings."

"I could give you a lift to work, if I'm organized in time. Some mornings can be chaotic."

"Thanks. The walk is okay. Besides, it's all down-hill." He moved into the living room, settling on the op-posite end of the sofa to Julia, next to his guitar. "I think there's a bus that runs from the wharf to the hospital and school up the road."

"It's probably a good idea to look up the timetable if you think you'll be without the Jeep for a while."

"True." He sipped his coffee, the warm liquid slid-ing down his throat. "The bus might be a viable option."

"I guess you may have to wait to book your Jeep in with your mechanic."

"Yep." He placed his mug on the coffee table and picked up his guitar and tuner. "Who knows how long I'll need to wait?"

She kicked off her shoes and tucked her feet under her body. "It sounds like you'll need a service done at the same time."

He nodded, plucking at the strings on his guitar. There was no way he could afford to pay for a comprehensive service anytime soon.

The large debt he owed Ryan from a few years ago still needed to be repaid. He could borrow more money from Ryan. Or repay less money to Ryan each fortnight from his church salary.

Sean had made the decision to repay his debt to Ryan as fast as possible. He was committed to standing on his own feet financially and taking responsibility for the way he managed his money. So far, he'd done okay, and he hadn't squandered his hard-earned dollars on unnecessary purchases.

The trip to Queensland had used up the small amount of savings he'd accumulated since starting his new job. There was nothing else to do but wait until he received his salary next week. He could walk to work and catch buses. And pray nothing else went wrong with the Jeep.

Chapter 10

A few weeks later, Julia jogged to the tennis court net. She leaned forward, knees bent, her body in the volley position. Her baseball cap shaded her face from the Saturday-afternoon sun. In the previous point, Sean had served a perfect ace deep into the backhand court, putting them in the lead in this game.

Her body pulsed with energy and anticipation of their imminent victory. They were playing in the semifinal of her interchurch competition, and had blitzed all the teams in the first round with the exception of Liam and Sally.

Julia held up her racquet, waiting for Sean to serve. Liam and Sally had beaten them in their first-round match and were playing their semifinal on the next court.

Sean's serve landed in the forehand court. Julia stayed at the net, smashing a winner into the far corner of the doubles court.

"Great shot." Sean gave her a high five on his way back to the baseline.

Her mouth curved into a wide smile, and she repositioned at the net for the next point. They were playing the best of four games, and were ahead two games to one. If Sean held his service game, they'd be through to the final.

Sean's serve flew past her, scoring an ace down the

center of the court. She saluted him, glancing over at the adjoining court. Liam and Sally shared a victory hug.

Frowning, she switched her attention back to her game. They were one point away from winning and competing against Liam and Sally in the final.

Sean sliced his serve wide into the backhand court. The receiver returned a soft shot to Julia. She volleyed the ball deep in the opposite corner, and their other opponent lobbed it back over the net. Julia let the ball bounce before hitting the winning shot down the line.

She raised her fist in victory, her heart rate accelerating. Sean jogged toward her, embracing her in a brief hug before they shook hands with their opponents.

She grinned, walking with Sean to the sidelines. "We made it through. I'm so excited to play in the final."

He nodded. "It's going to be a tough match, and we'll have to play a full set."

"Are you up for the challenge?"

"Yeah." He lowered his voice. "Our opponents in the final. Are they the couple who met with Simon just before my interview?"

"I'd wondered if you'd recognized Liam and Sally."

Sean grabbed his towel, wiping away the beads of sweat on his brow. "He doesn't look happy that he'll be playing against us."

Liam stared at them from across the court, arms crossed over his chest.

"Oh, well, he'll survive. He's probably worried that he could get beaten in the final like last time."

"Sally's a good player. I was watching their game earlier. They play in sync."

She nodded. "Her weakness is her net play, and her backhand isn't as strong as her forehand."

"You've been studying her play?"

"Of course. Liam has a nearly unplayable serve when he's on his game. And powerful ground strokes. We don't want to get stuck in any baseline rallies with him."

"Okay." Sean threw his backpack over his shoulder. "Who beat Liam and Sally last time?"

She lowered her gaze. "Actually, I was Liam's partner in the last tournament that he lost."

"Really? That puts a different spin on things. Did he dump you as a tennis partner for Sally?"

"Yes." She picked up her bag, meeting his gaze. "Liam and I were beaten by a couple at our church who were visiting from Florida. The score wasn't pretty. Liam was furious. He was determined to win next time."

Sean smiled. "Which is why you wanted to play with me. Are you holding a grudge over this?"

She walked up the steps to the clubhouse, evading his question. "I saw an opportunity to give us the best chance of winning. Don't forget, the prize is a free dinner tonight."

"Trust me, I haven't forgotten. And if we win, I'll feel as if I've earned every mouthful of my dinner."

She laughed. "Not if, but when. Losing today isn't an option. I know we can win, as long as we stay focused."

They shared a short refreshment break in the clubhouse before heading back on the court for the final game.

Julia waved to Liam and Sally, acknowledging Liam's cool response. He must be worried about losing. All day, he'd avoided her. She wasn't concerned by his aloof attitude, however.

Liam had become defensive as soon as he'd seen Sean in action, like an alley cat protecting his territory. Last weekend, Liam had bragged to one of her church friends that he and Sally were a sure thing to win today.

A smile touched her lips. She waited with Sean for the umpire to return to the court. A small crowd had gathered in the rows of seating outside the clubhouse looking down over their court.

Sean was a stronger player than Liam, with a more well-rounded game. She understood how Sean played. They anticipated each other's strokes, as if they'd played together for years.

The umpire tossed the coin and Liam won, electing to serve first. The score remained tied until the eleventh game, when Julia and Sean broke Sally's service game. Leading six games to five, Julia would be serving the next game for the set.

Sean walked beside her as they changed ends. "What's your plan?"

She slowed her pace, and adjusted her sunglasses. "Hit to Sally as much as possible. She's their weakest link."

"Will I see an ace from you?"

"Hardly. My serve's accurate, but not that fast. Unless you want me to aim for the line?"

"Go for it. We struggle when Liam returns your serve. Make him earn his cross-court winners."

"Okay, I'll mix it up with Sally. First serve to the backhand. When she moves to cover it, I'll go for her forehand."

"Deal." He stopped in the middle of the court. "We can do this."

"I know. I'm pumped and ready to go."

He grinned. "Good. Go whip them with your serve."

"I'll do my best." Julia wiped the perspiration from her brow, located a couple of tennis balls and prepared to serve to Liam. She put everything into her first serve, and it bounced outside the line.

She groaned. Not a good start to her service game.

Liam pounced on her slower second serve, smashing a cross-court winner. Love-fifteen.

Her strong first serve to Sally landed in the right spot. Sally returned a soft backhand and Sean attacked it at the net, slamming the ball down the line to win the point. Fifteen-all.

The game followed the same pattern, losing points to Liam and winning points from Sally until they reached deuce.

Julia swiped her sleeve over her forehead and lifted her damp ponytail off the nape of her neck. Her cotton tennis dress clung to the small of her back as she positioned herself to serve to Liam.

She'd played in the same tennis group with Liam for a few years and knew his game inside out. How could she surprise him and pull out a winner?

Liam shuffled toward his backhand, appearing to anticipate her serve down the middle of the court.

Her pulse raced, seeing her chance to angle for the forehand corner. She caught Sean's attention. He nodded, and she savored his encouraging smile. He believed in her. It was time to go for the big serve.

She sucked in a deep breath and served as hard as she could. The ball drilled deep into the forehand court. Liam got his racquet to the ball and kept it in play. Sean volleyed it back fast, and Sally missed the ball.

Julia jumped up and down, trying to suppress a squeal. They were one point away from victory. Sean gave her the thumbs-up, a big grin covering his face. He could probably taste their victory. The crowd on the sidelines hushed, waiting to see how the next point panned out.

Sally looked nervous, hovering around the baseline. Liam appeared to be barking instructions, which seemed to add to her anxiety. Julia had won the last two points from Sally's backhand return, and it looked as if Sally expected another cross-court serve.

Julia pelted her serve straight down the middle of the court, appearing to take Sally by surprise. Sally mis-timed her forehand and the ball sailed high through the air, landing behind the baseline next to Julia.

Julia let out a squeal. She ran to Sean. He hugged her, swinging her around in circles.

"We did it," he said. "Congratulations to us."

"I'm so happy!"

He set her on the ground and she stepped back, her heart overflowing with joy. She'd achieved her long-held dream of winning the competition.

They shook hands with Liam and Sally. Liam had a tight smile in place. Sally appeared close to tears.

Liam gave Sean a grim smile, sunglasses hiding his eyes. "You play well. Do you play in any of the local comps?"

"Thanks, and no, I don't play much tennis these days. I used to do the tournament circuit when I was a kid."

Julia lifted a brow. "Really? You never mentioned this before."

"My brother and I grew up playing tennis with our family. We had an excellent coach, a former pro player, who trained us well."

"Keep in touch," Liam said. "There's a men's dou-bles comp coming up soon. I'm looking for a partner, if you're interested."

Julia choked back a laugh. Liam was opportunistic, and plotting his next tournament win with Sean.

Sean grinned. "No problem. You can find me during the week at Beachside Community Church."

"Great." Liam grabbed Sally's hand. "You two enjoy your dinner prize tonight."

"We will," Julia said.

Sean draped his arm around Julia's shoulders, guiding her back toward the stairs leading to the clubhouse.

She leaned into his side, liking his closeness. "It's time to accept our winner's prize. They do a little ceremony thing."

"And afterward we can finally escape, and get ready for our exciting celebration dinner."

"Yep. I can't wait." She had chosen a dress to wear tonight, and looked forward to spending the evening with Sean.

Julia finished drying her hair. She pinned it up off her neck, allowing a few curls to escape around her face. She wore a sleeveless knee-length black dress for her dinner date with Sean.

The restaurant reservation was for eight, and Sean was due to pick her up in five minutes. She applied lipstick and mascara, and then put on her emerald necklace and earrings.

Her stomach grumbled. She gathered her purse and coat, ready for a delicious dinner. All the energy she'd expended on the tennis court had given her an enormous appetite.

Sean buzzed her intercom, and she went downstairs to greet him.

He waited outside the glass door at the main entrance to her apartment building.

Julia drew in a sharp breath, unable to tear her gaze away from him. He wore a stylish jacket, pants and polished leather shoes. She opened the door and stepped outside into the cool night air.

His eyes held an appreciative glint. "Wow, you look gorgeous."

Heat crept up her neck and face, his words warming her heart. "Thanks. This dress is one of my favorites." She slipped on her coat.

He escorted her to his Jeep. "I'm really looking forward to dinner."

"Me, too." She settled in her seat. The Jeep started on Sean's third attempt. "I thought the Jeep was fixed yesterday."

"They fixed the fan belt."

"Did they look at the starter and alternator? Or check that the battery's okay?"

He frowned. "It usually starts the first time, unless it's really cold."

Julia snuggled into her full-length coat, tucking her hands deep into her coat pockets. "It's a bit chilly tonight, and I think you should get it checked out if it keeps giving you trouble."

"I'll get it looked at soon." He revved the engine and drove along her street. "So far, so good."

She furrowed her brow. "Don't push your luck."

He shot her a bright smile. "You worry too much. Relax, the Jeep will be fine."

"Maybe, but I'd rather fix a problem now than have to deal with the consequences later." She found his laid-back attitude to life stressful, but now wasn't the time to have that particular conversation. They were on their way to the restaurant to celebrate their sweet victory.

"So you played representative tennis when you were younger?" she asked.

"Ryan and I played state level. He's a better player than me, and he was offered a place at the Institute of Sport."

"Wow, I had no idea he was that good."

"He hardly ever plays tennis these days. I think he prefers to go sailing on his yacht. I haven't beaten Ryan in a singles game for a long time, and I was impressed we could beat him and Cassie a few weeks ago."

"It was fun to beat them."

"You're also an excellent player."

She smiled. "I played at a regional level when I was at school, and A Grade until a few years ago."

"Why did you quit A Grade?"

"I started developing early signs of tennis elbow, and I didn't want to aggravate the problem by playing regular comps. Now I only play with the church crowd and go to the gym more often."

"I'm sorry about your injury. Did it give you any trouble today?"

She shook her head. "I'm careful not to play too often, and my strength training in the gym has helped."

"Good." He swung the Jeep into a parking space along the beachfront at Manly. "We could practice together sometime, as long as your elbow is okay?"

"Sure, but we can't be partners again in the comp until next year."

"How come?"

"It's one of the rules. They play three mixed doubles tournaments each year, and the same people can't win every tournament."

"That makes sense." He jumped out of the Jeep, headed around to her side and opened her door.

"Thanks." He reached for her hand and she twined her fingers with his. They crossed the road and walked along the footpath to the Italian restaurant. The cool sea breeze tickled her neck. She pulled up the collar of her coat.

He leaned closer, his voice gentle. "Are you warm enough?"

She nodded, pausing at the door to the restaurant. "But I'm looking forward to eating indoors."

A waiter led them to a secluded table near a window, which overlooked the beach and promenade.

Her mouth watered as she inhaled the pungent aroma of garlic bread and Bolognese sauce. A single candle burned in the center of their table. The atmosphere was set for romance.

Julia shivered. Tonight was turning into a real date. Sean looked fabulous in his tailored shirt, the top buttons left undone at his neck.

He passed her a menu, his fingertips skimming the back of her hand.

Her heart skipped a beat and she bent her head, reading the menu.

"What do you feel like?" he asked.

"Something filling. I'm starved."

"I have your favorite ice cream in my freezer at home. Do you want to come back to my place after dinner and practice for the concert?"

Her lips curved into a broad smile and she looked up from the menu. "You have the triple chocolate swirl?"

"An unopened tub."

"Okay. Count me in. I'm so hungry, I'm certain I'll have room for ice cream."

He grinned. "I'd forgotten how exhausting it is to play a full day of tennis."

They placed their pasta orders. During dinner, they chatted about their tennis win and the upcoming concert. Julia was enjoying herself—thanks to Sean's company and the delicious dinner. She took another bite, savoring the delicate flavors of the beef ravioli in a traditional Napoli sauce.

Sean finished his marinara pasta dish, a satisfied look on his face. "That was good. Would you like dessert? Tiramisu, *panna cotta*, gelato?"

She shook her head. "You've sold me on the ice cream. I know I've burned a lot of calories today, but I can't justify a double serving of dessert."

He laughed. "I have a confession. I bought the ice cream just in case we didn't win today. A consolation prize of sorts."

"Thank you. I don't buy it often because Billie and I lack self-control. We could eat the container between us in one sitting."

"You could finish the container tonight?"

She shook her head. "Two generous scoops will be plenty."

"That can be arranged." He stood, thrusting his arms into his jacket. "Let's get going."

At his apartment, Sean retrieved the ice cream from his freezer and two bowls from a cupboard. "Would you like a drink?"

"A hot chocolate would be nice."

He switched on the coffeemaker, and then placed two large scoops of ice cream into each bowl. "A third scoop?"

"No, thanks. I should probably have some self-control."

"Fair enough." He finished making her hot chocolate, and carried it into his living room.

She trailed behind with the ice cream bowls, and curled up beside Sean on the sofa. The ice cream melted on her tongue, sweet and creamy.

Sean picked up his guitar, tuning it while she ate her ice cream.

She licked her spoon. "Your ice cream is melting."

He passed her a copy of the sheet music. "I like it softer."

"Okay." She placed her empty bowl on the coffee table, and then scanned the words of the song. Sean savored his ice cream while she sipped her hot chocolate. They rehearsed "Amazing Grace" twice, the words from the famous hymn lingering in her mind.

She stood by the sofa, drinking in the superb evening view of the harbor. Lights twinkled on the distant horizon.

Sean leaned his guitar on the arm of the sofa and stood beside her, holding her hands. He stared into her eyes, his gaze intense. "That was brilliant."

She nodded, her pulse picking up speed. "You've nailed the music."

"And you're singing is exquisite." He lowered his head, his lips feathering a kiss on her closed mouth.

Her heart soared and she stepped closer, tilting up her chin.

His lips teased hers with light kisses, awakening feelings she could no longer ignore. She let go of his hands and parted her lips, resting the palm of her hand on his muscular chest. His hand cupped the back of her head, his fingers entwined in her hair. He deepened the kiss, his arm circling her body and drawing her closer.

Wow. She ran her hand through his lustrous hair, and her brain kicked into gear.

She pulled away, her breathing ragged. What had she done? Kissing Sean was a bad idea, but she couldn't deny her feelings. Or her longing to return to his arms.

Chapter 11

Sean held Julia's hand, his voice tender. "You're so beautiful."

She lowered her lashes. "Um, I think I should go home now." She let go of his hand and stumbled toward the front entry.

"Wait." He caught up with her at the door. "I need to drive you home."

"Oh, I forgot we came here in your Jeep." She collected her purse from the side table near the front door. "I could call a cab—"

"No, I'm happy to drive you home." And spend more time with her. Her soft lips captured his thoughts, and their sweet kiss had left him longing for more.

When she had looked up at him with her shimmering green eyes, he hadn't been able to resist claiming her lips.

He furrowed his brow. Had he made a mistake? Perhaps misread the situation and the intensity of her feelings?

They drove to her apartment in silence. He let the Jeep idle outside her building, unwilling to switch off the engine in case it wouldn't start again.

She glanced at him. "Thanks for dinner. And dessert."

"My pleasure, but I think we should talk about the kiss—"

"No." She twisted the strap of her purse around her fingers, staring at her lap.

"Why not?"

Her lower lip trembled. "I need time to think, to process what happened…"

He covered her hand with his, feeling her tension radiating through her fingers. "Julia, I care about you, and I want you to know that my feelings for you are genuine."

She looked up, her eyes soft. "I don't know what to say. You've become an important part of my life."

"We can take things slow."

She nodded, lacing her fingers through his. "Can you give me some time? This thing between us is, um, unexpected."

"Sure. I'm not going anywhere."

"Thanks." She released his hand and opened the passenger door.

Leaving the Jeep engine running, he strolled with her to the entrance of her building.

Her mouth curved into a small smile. "I'll be fine from here. And you shouldn't leave your Jeep unattended."

"Okay. Take care, and thanks for a great evening."

"It was fun." She paused on the threshold, her gaze riveted on him.

He stepped forward and brushed his lips over her cheek. "Sleep well."

"You, too." Her smile lit up her face, her eyes vibrant under the fluorescent outdoor lighting.

"You should go inside now. It's cold out here."

"Okay, see you later." She opened the door and entered the building.

He waited for her to start climbing the stairs before heading back along the path to his Jeep.

Sean drew in a deep breath. What had happened tonight? Their relationship had shifted to a different level, whether Julia was prepared to admit it or not.

He walked around to the driver's side of the Jeep, his step light. There had been an unexpected depth to their kiss, a strong emotional connection that he hadn't experienced before. The possibility of a future with Julia looked promising.

The next morning, Julia slept in late. She wandered into her kitchen, ready for breakfast. She rubbed her fingers over her face, hoping Billie wouldn't notice the dark circles rimming her blurry eyes.

Billie sat on a stool at their kitchen counter, wide-awake and eating a bowl of muesli. "Hey, Jules, what happened to you?"

Julia frowned, never having mastered the art of hiding her feelings from her sister. "I'm recovering from an exhausting day of tennis." And the emotional events that had followed after dinner with Sean.

Billie paused, her spoon midair. "Have you been crying? You look like you're upset."

"No, I'm really tired, that's all. I didn't sleep well." She'd tossed and turned in her bed until two or three, unable to settle. Her mind was still a jumble of confused thoughts and feelings regarding Sean.

Her sister arched a brow. "How was dinner last night? Was Sean as charming as ever?"

A wave of heat flooded her face, infusing her cheeks. "It was good. The food was great."

"Come on, you're holding out on me." Billie placed her index finger on her chin and squinted. "Something very interesting happened, or your face wouldn't be glowing."

Julia dropped a few slices of bread into the toaster, and

then poured a glass of orange juice. She remained silent for a couple of minutes while her sister tapped her finger expectantly. Finally, she said, "We had a nice dinner."

"And?" Billie grinned.

"And what?" The toast popped up. She grabbed the strawberry jam from the pantry and the butter from the fridge.

Billie gasped, clapping her hands together. "He kissed you, didn't he? That totally explains why you're acting like this."

"Acting like what?" She pulled out a stool and sat beside Billie, nibbling on a warm piece of toast.

"You never could hide anything from me. I know you too well. Now spill it and tell me all the juicy details."

She wrinkled her nose. "No way. I'm not saying anything because you'll make it into a big deal."

Her sister smiled. "So he did kiss you. I'd thought this might happen after seeing the warm looks he's been giving you these past few weeks."

"What warm looks?"

Billie rolled her eyes. "Anyone with eyes can see he's really into you. I think it's sweet."

"Okay, I admit it."

"Yes." Her sister's smile widened. "I knew I was right."

Julia sipped her juice. "But I'm not telling you any details, and I don't know where things are heading—"

"What?" Billie cradled her coffee mug in both hands. "Please tell me you didn't say it."

She lifted a brow. "Say what?"

"That you aren't interested in him and only want to be friends. Because that would be an outright lie."

Her stomach tightened. "I didn't really say much at all, other than I needed more time."

"Time for what? You have a gorgeous guy who is falling for you, plus you share similar interests."

"I said I needed time to think. And I don't need to be badgered about this by you, either."

Her sister shrugged. "I can't help it. I'm so excited you've found a great guy who shares your faith. What more could you want?"

Billie's question had kept her awake long into the night. She'd prayed about her growing feelings for Sean, unsure of what to do next.

She believed Sean had changed. She knew he was taking positive steps to improve his life. Also, Simon had developed a strong friendship with Sean, and spent a lot of time with him. The assistant pastor was a good judge of character.

In the short time she'd known Sean, she'd watched his faith grow and mature. He wasn't the same man she had first encountered at Ryan and Cassie's wedding.

Julia closed her eyes. *Please, Lord, give me wisdom.*

After everything Sean had been through, was it too soon for him to be embarking on a new relationship? Was he the right man for her?

The following afternoon, Julia returned to her reception desk at work with a tall latte. She had an hour left of work, and her energy levels were low.

Sean was in a meeting with Simon. She swallowed. It had been an interesting morning. She and Sean were both professional in their behavior and kept their focus on work issues, but she couldn't pretend there wasn't an underlying tension in their personal relationship. Even Simon had seemed to notice that something was up.

Julia scrunched her forehead, a headache starting to

throb in her temples. Two days after the kiss, and she was no closer to working out what she wanted, or didn't want.

She had skipped going to church last night, and only given Sean brief answers to his messages yesterday. Space to think was what she craved, but her work didn't allow her that particular luxury.

The sliding door opened and Billie entered the office. "Hi, Jules."

"Hey, what's up? What are you doing here?" Billie didn't visit her at work often, and she usually called first.

"Your letter has arrived." Billie fished an official-looking letter out of her purse. She handed it to Julia.

Her heart raced. The return address was from the government agency handling the adoption search.

She held the letter in her clammy hand, her mind whirling around the potential content. It was possible she would learn if her birth parents were alive, and whether or not they had agreed to be contacted.

"Hurry up and open it," her sister said. "I'm dying to hear what the letter says."

"I will." She ripped open the envelope and scanned the contents of the first page of the letter.

She gasped. "My birth mother is alive! She lives in Sydney and has consented to being contacted."

Billie grinned. "That's great news. I'm so excited for you. What about your birth father?"

She read further, flicking through the sheets of paper. "He's listed as unknown on my birth certificate."

"Oh." Billie paused. "What do you think that means?"

She frowned. "I don't know. Maybe this was a bad idea—"

"No, this is a good thing. You're finally going to have the opportunity to learn the truth about your heritage."

She nodded, hoping and praying Billie was right.

"Look," her sister said. "I have an appointment in ten minutes, so I must run. I had ducked home after lunch and, after checking the mail, thought I should get this to you as soon as possible. I had to wait for a cancellation to escape work."

"Thanks," Julia said. "I appreciate your bringing it over. You'd better hurry back to the clinic."

"I will. See you later tonight." Billie waved and rushed out the door.

Julia stared at the papers. *Lord, this is it, the day I've been waiting for, and hoping would bring me good news. Please help me to have the strength to face whatever lies ahead.*

Footsteps sounded in the hall and she glanced up. Sean ambled toward her, his gait relaxed. She stuffed the letter in her purse and switched her attention back to her computer screen.

He stopped beside her desk. "How's it going?"

"Fine." She attempted a smile. "I've nearly finished all my work for today."

He met her gaze, frowning. "Are you okay? Did something happen while I was meeting with Simon?"

"I'm a bit tired, that's all. I'll talk to you later."

He nodded. "We can talk now if it's important."

"No, it's okay. It can wait because I have a few things I should get finished before I leave today."

"Are you sure you don't want to leave early? I can look after everything here until five."

"Thanks, but no. I need to finish this report. Simon wants to look it over tonight."

"It can't wait until tomorrow?"

She shook her head. "His schedule is full tomorrow, and he needs it for a meeting on Wednesday."

The sliding door swished open and she turned around, her receptionist smile pasted to her face.

An attractive young blonde woman entered the office. She looked out of place, her makeup bold and her lean body encased in snug, fashionable clothes. The hem of her short skirt swirled around toned legs. An expensive gold watch encircled one of her thin wrists.

Sean stepped toward the woman, his eyebrows drawn together in a straight line. "Gemma, what are you doing here?"

Julia sucked in a deep breath, her attention fixed on Sean. He didn't look happy to see the blonde.

The woman gave Julia a cursory glance before returning all of her attention to Sean. "I'm glad I finally found you."

"Why?"

The blonde smiled, her perfect white teeth contrasting with her fire-engine-red lipstick. "We need to talk."

Sean's eyes widened. "I'm busy right now."

Julia's stomach constricted and she twirled a pen between her fingers. How did Sean know this woman?

Gemma placed a manicured hand on his forearm. "Please, it's important." She pouted, flicking her fingers through her flawless and stylish shoulder-length hair.

Sean removed Gemma's hand from his arm. He turned to Julia. "I need to take care of this. I'll be back before five."

Gemma huffed. "It will take longer than half an hour to discuss my little problem. Can't you just leave early and come back tomorrow?"

Julia straightened in her chair, disliking the distinctive purr in Gemma's voice. She appeared to be a woman who expected men to drop everything, and do whatever she wanted. And they probably did.

Sean cleared his throat. "Is that okay, Jules? I'll make up the time tomorrow." His eyes pleaded with her to understand that this was something he needed to do, rather than wanted to do.

Julia nodded, comforted by his use of her nickname in front of the blonde. "Sure. We can work out the details tomorrow."

Gemma grabbed hold of Sean's arm, shooting Julia a triumphant smile. "Thanks for understanding."

She stifled a groan, digging her fingernails into her palms. "You're welcome."

He nodded. "See you later."

Gemma tossed her hair back over her shoulders and walked out the door with Sean, remaining close by his side.

Julia chewed on her lower lip. Who was this Gemma woman? Why did Sean feel as though he had to do what she wanted? Did she have a hold over Sean?

New doubts avalanched down an icy slope in her mind. It was obvious Sean and Gemma shared some kind of history. How could she compete with a sophisticated blonde who looked like a catwalk model?

Julia dropped her head in her hands, a full-blown headache pounding her forehead. Did Sean have feelings for Gemma? Had he previously dated her or shared a romantic relationship with her?

Julia was jealous, and she could no longer deny her growing feelings for Sean. Or pretend her attraction to him wasn't important or real. What was he doing right now with the mysterious blonde, who obviously wanted something from him?

Chapter 12

Sean walked outside the church office and into the sun-dappled courtyard with Gemma.

He shrugged her hand off his arm. "What's going on?"

Gemma met his gaze. "I had to see you."

"Why?"

"It's important. Let's grab a coffee at the beach—"

"No." He shoved his hands on his hips. "What do you want?"

She batted her eyelashes. "It's complicated. I'm parched and I skipped lunch, so let's get out of here and find something to eat."

"I'm not going anywhere."

Gemma stared up at the towering brick church steeple, wrinkling her nose. "Churches make me nervous."

He let out a big breath. "We can talk here."

She shook her head. "I can't. God might hear me."

And she thought God wouldn't hear her at the beach? "Okay, we can go to the beach for a very quick chat."

"Thanks, Sean. This is really important."

He grunted. "It had better be." He walked beside her on the sidewalk, clenching his fists and moving his hand to stop her linking her fingers through his. They'd been close once, before he had turned his life around. Now she was like a stranger to him. He didn't belong in her world, and didn't want to play any role in her life.

They crossed the road to the promenade. He found a vacant bench facing the ocean and slouched back in the seat.

Gemma stood next to him, narrowing her eyes. "What about coffee?"

"We can talk here. I don't have time for coffee."

"Why not?"

"I want to return to work in five minutes. You'd better be quick."

She brushed sand off the wooden planks before perching on the edge of the bench, a look of distaste spreading over her face. A seagull approached her, and she glared at the bird.

Sean raised an eyebrow. "I don't have all day."

She folded her hands in her lap, her Gucci purse swinging on her shoulder. "I'd appreciate your help."

"Really? How did you find me?"

"Word gets around. I heard you'd gone religious." She raised her hand. "And before you start, you'd be wasting your time trying to convert me. I don't need religion."

He nodded, knowing she still believed money was all she needed. And her family had plenty of money. Just don't ask them how they made their fortune, and everything would be sweet.

"Anyway," she continued, "I miss you. Have dinner with me tonight, and I'll tell you in detail how you can help me out." She smiled. "You'll be fully compensated for your cooperation."

He cringed. "I can't help you. I'm not the same person you used to know."

Her smile waned. "Seriously, you're turning me down?"

He nodded.

"Are you crazy? My uncle said he could guarantee your assistance with this, um, delicate matter."

He froze, holding his breath for a long moment. They'd found him. If her uncle had tracked him down…

Gemma flicked her windblown hair off her face. "What do you say? Can we start negotiating terms?"

He crossed his arms over his chest. "No way. I'm out. I squared the ledger with your uncle. I owe him nothing. Didn't he tell you this?"

"Your brother evened the score by clearing your debt, but my uncle thought of you for this particular project."

"Gemma, I'm not getting involved. And I don't want to hear any details about the project." He ran his hands through his hair. "Can we forget this conversation ever happened? The last time I defied your uncle, I ended up in hospital."

She shrugged. "If you wish. I don't want to see you harmed."

He let out a deep breath. "Thank you. I'd also prefer you don't contact me again. I'm of no use to you or your uncle, and I think it's for the best if we go our separate ways."

She pouted, and trailed the tip of a glossy red finger-nail along his forearm. "If you insist."

He moved his arm out of her reach. "I do, and I mean it."

She handed over a hot pink business card. "My private phone number, if you change your mind…"

He shoved the card in his pocket, planning to throw it in the trash later. "Bye, Gemma."

"Ciao, sweetie." She blew him a kiss and walked away, her hips swaying and drawing the attention of a group of teen boys.

He sucked in a deep breath, expelling it slowly. He prayed her uncle would leave him alone. The ledger was squared. He owed the family nothing.

The waves rolled in, crashing against the sandy shore. He felt as though he'd been slam-dunked, shattered into tiny pieces like the grains of sand on the beach.

He'd read Gemma's angle and cut her off before she could try to lure him back into her family's illegal activities. He prayed her uncle was done with him and didn't want to renew their acquaintance. Gemma's family was trouble he didn't want or need ever again.

The next day, Julia arrived at the church office. Sean was already there. She checked the time on the wall clock. He had started work early. She greeted him, placed her morning coffee on her desk and opened the mail she'd collected from the church's postal box on her way to work.

Sean swung around in his seat and wheeled it over to her desk, sitting inches away from her. "How are you?"

"Fine." She didn't look up, continuing to organize the mail into piles on her desk.

"Look, I'm sorry I didn't make it back here before five yesterday."

She shrugged and sipped her coffee, the strong aroma helping her to wake up. "You said you weren't coming back. There's no need to apologize."

"The thing with Gemma. It wasn't the way it looked."

She paused, holding sheets of paper in the air. "Okay."

He looked her straight in the eye. "Don't you think I owe you some kind of explanation?"

"Not really." What a loaded question? She'd play it cool and try not to look bothered by the whole incident. "I'm not your keeper. It's not my business to know who you hang out with—"

"Hey, wait a minute. What exactly do you think happened yesterday between me and Gemma?"

She shrugged. "I've no idea." Her overactive imagination had conjured all sorts of scenarios last night. Most of them had made her feel uncomfortable or queasy.

"Gemma means nothing to me now."

"Oh, then, I guess she did mean something to you at some point in time."

He dropped his gaze. "I knew her in Melbourne a few years ago."

"Oh, I didn't realize you lived in Melbourne."

"Yeah, it's a time in my life I'd rather forget."

"Was this before you reconnected with Cassie and Ryan?"

"Yep. I moved back to Sydney from Melbourne. Do you remember hearing about how I had gotten beaten up in the city and Ryan drove me to the hospital?"

She nodded. "What has that got to do with this girl?"

"Her uncle ordered the beating."

Julia gasped, covering her mouth with her hand. "Why?"

"I owed him money, and I didn't pay up in time."

"That's scary." Sean had ended up in the hospital and, with Ryan and Cassie's assistance, he'd agreed to seek help for his gambling problem. That one event had been the catalyst that had turned his life around. "Please tell me you don't still owe her uncle money."

He shook his head. "I owe them nothing. Gemma wanted to catch up and reconnect, but I convinced her it would be a bad idea."

She let out a deep breath, relieved he wasn't planning to see Gemma again. "How did she find you?"

"I don't know. She mentioned her uncle during our conversation, and I suspect he tracked me down."

Her mouth fell open. "Do you think you're in danger?"

"Nope."

"Are you sure?"

"Gemma was scoping to see if I was interested in hanging out with them again, but I made it crystal clear I wanted nothing to do with her or her family."

She frowned. "I hope you didn't offend her. What if she tells her uncle you rejected her…"

"It's okay. I was diplomatic, and I know how to handle her."

Her stomach clenched. "I'm sure you do." No doubt Gemma had fallen for his charm. She didn't want to think about her anymore. The whole situation drew out emotions she wasn't ready to process.

He raised an eyebrow. "She won't cause me any trouble."

Julia attempted a smile, lightening her tone. "I hope you're right." Time to change the subject. "Last night I wrote a letter to my birth mother."

"That's great. So you've decided you want to meet her?"

She nodded. "She lives in Sydney, which makes it easier. But I haven't told Billie I've written the letter and initiated contact with my birth mother."

"Why? I thought she was excited for you."

"The thing is, she's heard nothing from her search. She lodged her application before I even started mine. Plus, she's the one who is desperate to contact her birth parents."

"Okay. That makes sense. Do you think she'll be upset if she learns you're moving forward with your search?"

"Sort of. She dropped the subject after talking about our search all the time before I got the letter."

He frowned. "Are you going to tell her about the letter you wrote soon?"

"I don't know. I don't want to hurt her unnecessarily. Maybe if I wait until she hears news about her search..."

"I thought you wanted Billie with you when you meet your birth mother for the first time. Didn't you have it all worked out?"

She nodded. "I don't really want to do it by myself."

"I'll go with you."

She met his steady gaze. "Really?"

He smiled. "It's a big moment, and scary because you don't know what will happen. I'd hate to see you have to do it by yourself."

"Thank you." She stared into the sparkling depths of his eyes. "This means a lot to me."

"I know. You have my word I'll be there for you."

She blinked away the moisture building between her lashes. *Lord, thank You for bringing Sean into my life. I'm petrified to meet my birth mother, but I know You'll be with me, whatever happens.*

The fear that held her heart captive had loosened its grip. She wouldn't have to do this alone.

The following Sunday evening, Sean strummed the final note on his guitar for the last song of the service. Simon returned to the stage at the front of Beachside Community Church to deliver his closing remarks.

Sean's gaze scanned the congregation, and he spotted his parents sitting near the back. He hadn't noticed them earlier. They must have slipped into their seats during the service.

He'd expected them to arrive earlier in the day, but they'd been delayed, giving him a chance to do a big cleanup in the apartment. This time his father wouldn't be able to criticize his lack of housekeeping skills.

Tonight was the first time he'd seen his father since they'd had breakfast after their disastrous confrontation at the launch party. His mother had said she'd been working on his dad. Sean wondered if his father's attitude had improved.

The service ended. Julia started packing up the sound equipment beside him.

She smiled at him. "Are you staying for coffee?"

"I don't know. My mom and dad are here." His parents were headed in his direction, walking down the center aisle.

"Has anything changed with your dad?"

"I'll find out soon enough, because they're less than six feet behind you."

Julia turned and greeted his parents.

Sean gave his mom a hug, and held out his hand to his father.

His dad's handshake was firm and a slight smile tilted up his lips. "You played well tonight, son."

Sean raised an eyebrow, shooting his mom a quizzical look. "Thanks, Dad. The band always sounds good."

His mother's smile widened. "It's great to see you involved in church, Sean. Isn't it, Brian?"

His father nodded. "It's good to know those guitar lessons I paid for all those years ago weren't wasted."

"Absolutely not," Julia said. "Sean's an excellent guitarist."

"I agree," his mom said.

"Sean, I can pack up your equipment so you can leave now with your folks."

"Thanks," he said. "Unless, Mom and Dad, you'd like to stay for coffee?"

His mom shook her head. "I'd prefer to go back to the apartment, if that's okay. Our computer at home is broken and I need to do a few things online."

He frowned. "Do you need the computer back? I can use my phone if I need to go online."

His father nodded. "That would be a great help. We'll bring it back as soon as our main computer is fixed."

"I appreciate your loaning me your spare computer."

"You're welcome." His mom turned to Julia. "I hope we can catch up with you this week, maybe dinner at Sean's place?"

Julia smiled. "I'd like that."

He met Julia's gaze, his heart warming. "We'll have to line up a time when you're free."

"I think I'm free most nights. Anyway, I'll see you tomorrow morning, and we can work out the details."

"No worries." He waved goodbye to Julia before moving into the crowded aisle with his parents.

His mother linked her arm through his, leaning in close. "She's a lovely girl."

"I know."

She lifted a brow. "Are you two dating?"

"Not exactly, and nothing is official. Before you say anything, I'm happy with the way things are developing."

His mom grinned. "I'm so pleased. I really like her. And she's a good influence on you, as well."

His father wrinkled his forehead. "What are you talking about?"

"Sean and Julia," she said.

"I still think she's too good for you," his father said.

"Now, Brian, I told you to keep your opinion to yourself."

He nodded. "Son, I hope it works out for you."

Sean's jaw dropped. "Seriously?"

"She's a great girl. And, as your mother pointed out, you could do much worse. I really like her, too."

Sean smiled. "Thanks, Dad."

Wow, what had happened? Where had his grumpy, disapproving father gone?

Lord, thank You for answering my prayer. Please help me to work on improving my relationship with Dad.

Chapter 13

On Saturday afternoon, Julia sat beside Sean in the grandstand at Manly Oval. The charity-concert dress rehearsal had started an hour ago. She tucked a few strands of hair behind her ears that had blown loose from her ponytail in the gusty sea breeze. A group of schoolchildren performed an Aussie bush ballad song on the makeshift stage in front of the goal posts.

She wriggled in her seat, her stomach tense. "We're up soon."

Sean nodded, his left hand balancing his guitar case, which leaned on a vacant fold-down seat beside him. "Do you feel ready?"

"I think so. We've rehearsed the song plenty of times."

"We should do okay. Those kids on stage are cute."

"I like their period costumes."

"A nice touch. Do you want to dress up?"

She laughed, shaking her head. "What would we wear? The concert is only a few weeks away." The kids filed off the stage, and a drama troupe moved into position.

"It's a bit late notice. Maybe next time."

"Yep." Julia sipped her bottled water. A crowd had gathered at the oval. She was encouraged to see so many people had donated their time to support the charity event for homeless people.

Their names were called over the loudspeaker, and she walked with Sean to the edge of the stage. Volunteers holding clipboards raced around behind the stage, organizing the performers to keep the rehearsal running on schedule.

Soon, she was onstage with Sean, feeling the gaze of the crowd upon her. She closed her eyes, praying and listening for Sean's guitar lead-in.

As he played the opening riff, she relaxed, the words from "Amazing Grace" clear in her mind. Her voice soared, and she hit all the notes at the right time. Minutes later it was over, and she hurried off the stage with Sean.

He grinned. "It went well."

She nodded. "I tried to forget there were so many people watching us."

"You did great. This crowd is nothing compared to the number of people they're expecting here on the day."

She strolled with Sean toward the car park. "I'm trying not to think about it."

"We'll be fine, and it's for a good cause."

"True." She was glad to be involved in this important ministry. Her heart yearned to do more of God's work, but she hadn't discerned any clear direction for the future.

She'd investigated overseas missionary opportunities. But now that she'd initiated contact with her birth mother, she wasn't sure if she wanted to live overseas for an extended period of time.

Confused, she'd sought direction during her daily prayer time. Her current employment contract with Beachside ended soon. Then what? She had no firm plans for the future.

They approached the exit to the oval.

Sean stopped beside her, and pointed to a table on their

left. "They have a signup sheet for volunteers at their soup kitchen. I think I'll put my name down."

"Sounds like a great idea."

"I've been thinking about how I can contribute, and I can sort of relate to the issues these people may be confronting."

"That makes sense." Sean had shared how he'd stayed with friends and had no fixed address when his gambling addiction and associated debts were spiraling out of control. "How about you?" He looked her straight in the eye. "You said you wanted to do ministry work. Is this the kind of thing you had in mind?"

She twisted her hands together. "To be honest, I've no idea what I want to do. A few months ago, I thought I had it all planned out, but now…"

"I'll pray for you," he said.

She smiled. "Thanks. I need it."

"We all do." He shoved his hair off his forehead. "I've learned a lot about prayer over the past couple of months."

She nodded.

"Can you wait for me while I sign up? It won't take long."

"Sure." Sean headed over to the table, and the words from "Amazing Grace" drifted into her mind. Sean appeared to get the whole grace thing, understanding his need for Jesus as his Lord and savior. During the week, he'd shared how he'd finally, eight months ago, understood why trying to be a good person wasn't enough.

Julia sucked in a deep breath. She'd spent years doing good deeds to prove to God she was worthy. And she'd felt superior to those who had failed to meet God's standards as laid out in the Bible, not realizing her pride in her achievements was a stumbling block in her own faith.

Lord, forgive me. Forgive my arrogance in believing I was a better person than Sean. Help me to live my life in a way that is pleasing to You.

Marrying a pastor was not going to improve her status with God, who loved her despite her failings. How could she have sat in church for so many years and not fully understood God's grace?

She shook her head, sorrow falling on her shoulders like snowflakes building into a raging storm. She'd judged Sean. Ignored her own shortcomings. Now she was in awe over the maturity she'd witnessed in his faith journey. She could learn a lot by following his example.

A week later, Julia arrived home from work carrying a box of Chinese takeout for dinner. She should be going to the gym, but she'd decided she wanted a night off to chill, maybe read a book.

She threw the mail she'd collected from her letterbox on the kitchen counter and switched on her coffeemaker. She slid onto a stool and flicked through the mail, stopping when she spotted a letter addressed to her in unfamiliar handwriting.

Could it be from her birth mother? The timing made sense.

She ripped open the envelope, scanning the single sheet of stationery inside. Her heart raced. Amanda Coles. The name listed on her birth certificate. Amanda wanted to set up a meeting with her soon, and had provided a contact phone number.

Julia held her breath for a long moment, glad that Billie was out for the evening and had forgotten to check the mail. Her sister awaited news on her birth parent search, and Julia had put off telling Billie about the progress she'd made. Now that the letter had arrived, she'd have to inform Billie and her parents soon.

She stared at the phone number—her link with the woman who had given birth to her. What would she sound like on the phone? Would Amanda's voice be similar to her own?

She dialed the number before she had a chance to think and lose her courage. The dial tone buzzed on, and she waited for someone to pick up the call.

The call diverted to voice mail. Julia left a breathless message, including her name and number.

She disconnected the call and slumped on the stool, staring at her takeout. Her stomach was on a roller coaster, too churned up to welcome food.

When would her birth mother return her call? Tonight? Tomorrow? She could switch off her phone and let the call go to voice mail.

Julia poured a cup of coffee. She daydreamed about the perfect reunion. She'd fall in love with her birth mom straight away. Amanda would be delighted to meet her, and would arrange a family dinner, possibly in her home. Julia would meet the family. They'd all get along.

Dark thoughts intruded on her happy daydream. Why wasn't her father's name listed on her birth certificate? This was one question she wanted to ask if she had the opportunity to meet her birth mother in person.

The next day, Julia sat at her desk and tried to focus on editing the document on-screen. Her concentration was shot, and she'd already missed two obvious typos. Even her midmorning extrastrong cappuccino hadn't helped her keep her mind on the task.

Sean swung around in his chair, as if sensing her uneasiness. "I finished the website updates."

"Great." When would her birth mother contact her? All evening yesterday she'd kept her cell phone close by, anticipating the phone call from Amanda.

He frowned. "What's up?

"I'm a little distracted today." She flicked her pen between her fingers. "I might take an early lunch."

"Sure, I wasn't planning on lunch until after one."

"Okay." Her cell phone vibrated, Unknown Number listed as the caller ID on the screen. She answered the call.

"Is this Julia Radcliffe?" a woman asked.

"Yes, I'm Julia." Ugh, she hoped it wasn't a telemarketing call.

The woman cleared her throat. "My name is Amanda Coles."

She gasped. "Hi, Amanda. You got my message."

"Yes, um, I had some personal issues to deal with yesterday, and I didn't get a chance to return your call."

She frowned. Personal issues? Wouldn't her situation with her natural daughter also be considered a personal issue? Amanda's voice was strained, as if she was holding back something important.

"That's okay," Julia said. "I'm glad to hear from you."

"You mentioned in your letter you'd like to meet me in person."

"Yes, please. That is, assuming this is something you want…"

"Of course. I live on the other side of town, but I'm sometimes in Neutral Bay on the weekend. Would a meeting in Neutral Bay on a Saturday morning be convenient?"

"Absolutely. Name the date and time, and I'll be there."

They arranged a meeting in two weeks at a Neutral Bay café. Amanda ended the call, her tone abrupt and lacking warmth.

Julia stared at her phone, chaotic thoughts and doubts swirling in her mind.

Sean patted her shoulder. "Are you sure you're okay?"

She shook her head, fighting back the tears threatening to form in her eyes. "That was my birth mother."

"Oh." He paused. "The call didn't go well."

She nibbled her lower lip. "Sort of. I don't know. Maybe my expectations are too high?"

He raised an eyebrow, concern shadowing his eyes. "What do you mean?"

"She's like a stranger."

His eyes softened and he held her hand. "Well, that's kind of true. You haven't seen her since you were a small baby."

"I know, but I thought I'd feel something." She lowered her lashes, blinking away the moisture in her eyes. "Some kind of connection, since she did once carry me inside her body."

"Oh, Jules." He gave her an affectionate hug. "Give it time. Is this the first time you've spoken with her?"

She nodded, liking the feel of his cotton shirt against her cheek.

"Don't be too quick to pass judgment. Wait until you've met her in person and talked to her."

She moved out of his embrace, leaning back in her chair. "Thanks. I feel a little bit better."

"Good." He smiled. "And I'll be there with you, holding your hand when you meet her in Neutral Bay."

She nodded, attempting to smile. "Don't you have your men's breakfast group on Saturday mornings?"

"We usually finish up by ten at the latest. I'll have plenty of time afterward to get to the café."

"Are you sure? I can pick you up on the way."

He shook his head. "I don't want to inconvenience

you, and I'll make sure I leave plenty of time to get there. You have my word."

She smiled. "Thank you. I appreciate this, and my next job is to break the news to Billie and my parents."

A task she wasn't looking forward to. She anticipated problems, assuming her parents and sister wouldn't take the news well. Her mother, in particular, was still having a hard time dealing with this issue.

Lord, help me to be gentle when I speak with my family. And to have an open mind when I meet Amanda.

A deep sense of foreboding filled her mind. As much as she wanted her meeting with Amanda to go well, she feared she wouldn't like what she discovered. Her idealistic dreams could be shattered into minuscule pieces.

Chapter 14

Two weeks later, Sean walked at a brisk pace to his apartment building. It was faster to walk to and from the men's breakfast held at a home in a nearby street than to drive and try to find a parking space.

He glanced at his watch, frustrated that he couldn't find his phone earlier this morning. The missing phone must be somewhere in his apartment. He'd tried calling his phone from the home phone Ryan had kept connected, but his cell had never rung. The battery must be dead.

He'd left the men's breakfast group early, wanting to ensure he arrived in Neutral Bay in plenty of time to support Julia during her first meeting with her birth mother. She had sounded stressed and nervous when he'd spoken with her last night on his now misplaced phone.

He ducked upstairs in the elevator, deposited his Bible on the side table inside his apartment and grabbed his keys for the Jeep. Within minutes, he was in the parking garage, ready to battle the Saturday-morning traffic to Neutral Bay.

Sean turned over the engine, and it refused to start. He tried a second time. Nothing. *Lord, please, I really need the Jeep to start today.*

Three more attempts to start the engine failed. His

pulse rate accelerated, a new burst of adrenaline kicking in. No, this couldn't be happening. Not today, of all days.

He thumped the steering wheel, his hand stinging from the impact. The starter motor was broken. Silence hung over him in the cabin of the Jeep like a suffocating cloak. He turned the key in the ignition. No response.

What was Julia's phone number? He leaped out of the Jeep and raced back upstairs. It started with zero four zero, then something. If only he'd written the number down somewhere and not relied on his phone's speed dial.

He groaned, knowing he couldn't even send her an email. His parents still hadn't returned the computer.

Ryan. His brother should have Julia's number. He dialed Ryan's phone. The call went straight to voice mail.

He muttered a few choice words under his breath. Ryan was travelling overseas today for a work trip. He couldn't remember Cassie's number, but he knew their home phone number. Would she be there this morning?

Sean called Cassie, the repetitive dial tone droning on and on. The call went to voice mail, and he pressed his thumb down hard on the end key. He raked his hand through his hair, out of ideas on how to contact Julia. Her number was unlisted, and he'd never seen an old-fashioned paper phone directory in the apartment, if they still existed.

He let out a big breath, and dialed the easy-to-remember number for a cab. The company placed him on hold in a queue. He tapped his fingers on the kitchen counter. He spoke into the handset and entered his trip details. The computer voice promised a cab in ten to fifteen minutes.

Sean checked the clock again, his heart sinking faster than a boulder landing in a pond. There was no way he'd make it to the café in Neutral Bay in time. He'd already lost at least half an hour trying to start the Jeep and coming up with an alternative plan.

He dropped into a lounge chair and closed his eyes, the enormity of his latest debacle registering in his mind. Julia would be at the café soon, and he was going to no-show if he didn't get moving and wait downstairs.

He closed his eyes, covering his face with his hands. *Lord, I've messed up big time. Please be with Julia as she goes it alone because of my mistakes. I pray she will forgive me for letting her down when she needed me most.*

Julia made her way through the busy Neutral Bay café to a vacant table with a clear view of the entrance. Ten minutes early for her first meeting with her birth mom, she sat in an uncomfortable wooden chair and tightened her grip on her purse.

She ordered a latte, hoping the coffee would help calm her tumultuous stomach. The day she'd been waiting for had arrived.

She sucked in a steadying breath and ran her fingers through her hair. The café was close to full capacity, with a number of patrons enjoying brunch.

Her gaze remained fixed on the door. She had no idea what Amanda looked like, and it hadn't crossed her mind to ask about her appearance during their brief phone conversation a few weeks ago.

A middle-aged woman entered the café. Her bleached-blond hair and weathered complexion didn't fit the profile of the average customer in the chic café, despite her neat appearance and slim physique.

Julia glanced at a clock on the wall. Where was Sean? He'd promised he'd be here before ten-thirty, and he hadn't sent her a message to let her know he'd be late.

The blonde woman turned in her direction, and Julia stared into a pair of hard green eyes identical to her own.

She gasped, covering her mouth with her hand. This woman must be her birth mother. The woman walked toward her and smiled, displaying yellowed teeth. A couple were missing.

Julia clenched her hands together in her lap, forcing her own mouth into a polite smile. "Hi, you must be Amanda."

The woman nodded and extended her hand. "So you're Julia."

Julia shook her birth mother's wrinkled and calloused hand. How old was Amanda? The lines on her face and sallow complexion suggested she was in either in her late fifties or sixties, or had lived a tough life.

Her stomach sank, suspecting the latter was the truth.

Amanda sat opposite Julia. "You found the café okay?"

She nodded and thanked the waiter for her latte. "I've been here before."

Amanda placed her coffee and cake order. "My colleagues often meet here."

Julia requested a slice of New York cheesecake. She needed something sweet to help her get through this meeting. Where was Sean? "What type of work do you do?"

Amanda fidgeted with an amethyst ring on her right hand. Her left hand was bare. "I'm a drug and alcohol counselor."

She lifted an eyebrow, her curiosity aroused. Was her birth mother a former addict? "An interesting career choice."

Her birth mom frowned. "Let's cut to the chase. You look as if you've lived a pretty comfortable life."

She nodded. "My parents have been good to me."

"I'm glad things worked out well for you. Looking at you now, I know I made the right decision back then."

"Did you have doubts?" Julia nervously sipped her latte.

"Of course. Over the years I've wondered how you were doing. I had hoped you were happy and had a nice life."

"What happened back then?"

"With you?"

She nodded. Chaotic thoughts danced through her mind. Would she learn the truth today?

Her cell phone beeped, and she scrambled through her purse to check the message. She read the brief text from Cassie. Why hadn't Sean contacted her?

The waiter returned with their order, and Amanda picked at her slice of carrot cake. "I was fifteen when I became pregnant with you."

Julia paused, her spoonful of cheesecake mid air. "You were so young."

"In some ways. I'd been living on the streets since I was fourteen."

Her mouth gaped. "What about your parents?"

"My mother…" She coughed, and sipped her coffee to clear her throat. "Your grandmother was a hippie and I never knew my father. I refused to go to school. She kicked me out of home and disappeared. Years later I learned she'd moved to Nimbin."

Tears pricked Julia's eyes. "What happened next?"

"You were born. I gave you up for adoption. My life went downhill, big-time."

"I'm sorry to hear this. It must have been so hard for you."

She nodded. "Are you sure you want to hear more? My story isn't pretty."

"Go on." She braced her back, preparing to hear the more details.

"Heroin became my best friend and worst enemy for over two decades." Amanda ate another mouthful of cake. "I've been sober five years and ten days."

Julia blinked, unable to look at the woman sitting across from her. Never in her wildest dreams had she imagined hearing this story from her birth mom. She struggled to comprehend the implications of Amanda's words.

Amanda tapped her fingers on the table. "Don't waste your tears on me."

She looked up, her gaze honing in on Amanda's gap-toothed grin. "You're okay now?"

Her birth mother laughed, dropping her head back and ignoring the pointed stares from patrons at nearby tables. "Look, Julia, you can't expect to be okay after abusing your body for two decades." She leaned forward in her seat, lowering her voice. "I have hep C and my liver is a mess. The doctors say I'm on borrowed time."

A single tear trickled out of the corner of Julia's eye. "You're serious?"

"Deadly serious." Her mouth flattened into a grim line. "The meds help, but I have a death sentence."

"I'll pray for you."

Amanda scowled. "Fat lot of good that will do."

"No, I'll pray for you every day."

She waved her hand through the air. "Don't waste your time. I don't believe in God."

Julia felt like someone had slid a knife into the core of her heart. "No way. What do you believe will happen after you die?"

"Nothing." She drained her coffee mug. "My miserable, rotten life will come to an end, and that's it."

"I disagree. I hope we can talk about this——"

"No. I don't want to hear." She scraped her chair back and stood. "I have an appointment in five minutes." She slapped some cash on the table. "I'll leave you now, so you can digest what you've learned."

"Wait." She glanced past Amanda.

Sean rushed toward her. She glared at him before returning her attention to Amanda. "I want to see you again."

"Sure. We could meet here next month."

She stood and Sean moved to her side. "Where have you been?"

"I can explain," he said.

Amanda frowned. "Is he your boyfriend?"

Sean narrowed his eyes as he took in Amanda's appearance. "I'm Sean," he said, extending his hand.

"Amanda." She shook his outstretched hand, then turned to Julia. "I've got to go. Call me to arrange our next meeting."

"Sure. But I have one more question."

"Shoot."

"Do you know who my birth father is?"

Amanda sighed. "I haven't a clue. That time in my life is a blur, and I knew a lot of boys back then."

Julia gulped, pushing down the burning emotion building inside her. "Thanks for telling me the truth."

"What would I gain by lying?" Her gaze softened. "You take care, okay?"

She nodded, watching her birth mom leave the café.

Sean reached for her hand, and she wrenched her fingers out of his grasp.

"Where have you been?"

"Calm down. I can explain——"

"Don't you dare tell me to calm down." Fierce anger

rose to the surface as she rifled through her purse to cover her share of the bill.

"What happened?"

"You'd know exactly what happened if you'd been here when you said you would." She left some cash on the table and stormed out of the café.

Sean followed a few steps behind, running to catch up with her. "Hey." He reached for her arm.

"Don't touch me." Pulse racing, she edged away from him. "Leave me alone."

She stepped onto the busy street, and a BMW slammed on the brakes, the driver honking his loud horn multiple times.

Sean pulled her back onto the sidewalk. "Jules, you need to calm down." He looked her straight in the eye. "Where's your car?"

She searched the street, her mind drawing a blank. "Somewhere near here. I had to drive around before I found a spot."

"Okay, let's sit on the bench under the tree, and you can gather your thoughts."

She slumped onto the bench, sucking in a few shallow breaths. This couldn't be happening. This morning must be a bad nightmare that she'd awaken from soon.

"Jules, look at me." Sean sat beside her, his eyebrows drawn together. "Please talk to me."

She rubbed her hands over her eyes, clearing the moisture from her lashes. Her mind scrambled to put her disjointed thoughts into words. "How could you?"

"What?"

"Leave me to deal with this by myself."

He frowned. "Deal with what? Tell me what happened."

"It's a mess. A disaster, and I never should have let Billie talk me into doing this."

"It'll be okay," he said, a soothing tone in his voice. "We know God has it all under control."

"No, he doesn't."

He paused, his frown deepening. "What do you mean?"

"It won't be okay."

"Why? What did she say to you?"

She met his gaze, moisture filling her eyes and pain twisting her heart. "She's dying and she doesn't believe in God."

Chapter 15

Sean lurched back on the bench, feeling like he'd been soccer punched in the gut. "What did you say?"

Her beautiful green eyes brimmed with tears. "She has no faith, and she's dying."

His eyes widened. "How? Has she got cancer or something?"

She shook her head. "Hep C." Her voice broke. "She was a heroin addict for years."

"Oh, Jules, I'm so sorry." He gathered her close, and she relaxed in his embrace. He patted her shoulder and whispered soothing words in her ear.

She pulled back and wiped away her tears with the back of her hand. Her glittering eyes met his gaze. "Please answer my question. Where were you earlier when I needed you?"

"The Jeep wouldn't start this morning. I walked home from the men's breakfast group with plenty of time to drive here."

She shook her head. "You told me you were getting it fixed."

"I know, I just hadn't got around to doing it. I don't know what went wrong today. I called a cab, but had to wait for it to arrive, and then the traffic was heavy..."

She threw her hands in the air. "I don't believe it. I

trusted you to be here. I could have picked you up on my way and not had to do this all by myself."

The accusation in her voice stung. His excuse was lame. How could he make this situation right and convince her he'd done everything he could to get here, only to find out he was too late?

He took a deep breath. "I'm sorry—"

"What?" She leaped to her feet, hands on hips. "You think you can just apologize and make this better?"

He stood, unsure of what to say next. He'd never seen Julia lose control, had no idea her cool exterior hid a volatile temper. "Look, I admit I messed up—"

"Yeah, you messed up, all right." She glared at him, eyes blazing. "Why didn't you call me?"

He swallowed. "I've lost my phone. I think it's in the apartment somewhere, and the battery must be dead because I tried ringing it. No sound."

"Unbelievable. Why didn't you call me from your home phone? You managed to call a cab okay."

He rubbed his hands over his face, walking a few steps until he stood behind the bench. "I couldn't find your number anywhere. I went downstairs straight away so I wouldn't miss the cab."

She crossed her arms over her chest. "You don't know my number?"

He swallowed again. Hard. "I have you at the top of my speed-dial list. Do you know my number?"

She rattled off his cell phone number and home number without any hesitation.

He stared at the ground, the stone paving uneven and worn with age. "I said I'm sorry. What more do you want?"

"Nothing. I can't trust you to keep your word. If I'd known you hadn't fixed the Jeep…"

He sucked in a deep breath. "There's a reason the Jeep wasn't fixed."

"This had better be good."

Or what? He swallowed his pride and blurted out the truth. "I didn't have enough money to pay for a new starter motor."

She frowned. "What have you been doing spending money on me when you needed to fix the Jeep?"

"I care about you. I wanted to spend time with you, spoil you."

She shook her head. "You don't get it. Money doesn't mean anything to me."

"You can't be serious?" He leaned forward, his hands resting on the back of the bench. "Money must mean something to you. You go to work and earn a salary."

She stood in front of him, the bench seat separating them. "I have a trust fund. I choose to work, but I don't need a job to pay my bills."

His mouth gaped, his heart deflating. She was loaded, and he had never known. Not that it would change how he felt about her.

Waves of inadequacy rolled over him. She was rich, and he had nothing but an unquenchable desire for wealth that had gotten him into serious trouble in the past.

He cleared his throat. "Now you know the truth about me. My dad's right. You're too good for me, and all I ever do is let you and other people down. I know my apology isn't enough, but I don't know what else I can do."

She slumped on the bench and buried her head in her hands. She sobbed, her shoulders shaking and her breathing erratic.

He sat beside her for a few minutes, giving her the space to let all the emotion out. He'd messed up earlier, but he now had an opportunity to look after her and show her how much he cared.

"Jules, I'm driving you home."

She looked up, her red-rimmed eyes widening. "I can drive myself."

He frowned. "Not in the state you're in. Let me help you."

She shrugged. "If you wish."

"I do."

She handed her car keys to him and stood. "I'm pretty sure I parked my car in the next street."

"Okay." He walked beside her in silence.

She seemed lost in her thoughts, deep frown lines appearing between her brows.

After making himself comfortable in the driver's seat, he wove her Honda through the heavy traffic. She tuned the radio to a local station, and he listened to the music as it filled the silence.

They reached the cars queuing at the Spit Bridge and he brought the Honda to a halt, switching off the engine. The antiquated bridge rose, allowing yachts to pass through to Middle Harbour.

She unbuckled her seat belt. "I'll drive now."

He touched her hand briefly. "Are you sure?"

She nodded. "I'll drop you home at your place."

He got out of the car and they swapped seats. Julia adjusted the driver's seat and mirrors. The bridge lowered, and the drivers ahead turned on their engines, ready to continue their journey across the bridge to the northern beaches.

She joined the crawling vehicles, her gaze fixed on the road.

He stayed quiet, aware she had no intention of talking to him. He struggled to imagine how difficult this morning had been for her. He wished he could turn back the clock and start the day over.

Lord, I've let her down and hurt her at a time when she needs the people who care for her to be there for her. Forgive me for my foolishness, and my lack of responsibility in maintaining the Jeep. Please help Julia to forgive me, and let me prove to her that I love her and have her best interests at heart.

Julia swung her car into a parking space outside his apartment building, letting the engine idle.

He stared at her stiff profile and the straight line of her mouth. "Thanks for the lift." He paused. "And I'm sorry about everything."

She didn't respond, her body rigid.

He opened the passenger door.

"Wait." Her mouth softened. "I need time alone. Time to think and process what I've learned today."

He nodded. "Are you still up to performing at the concert tonight?"

"Yep."

He walked away, his heart tearing apart inside him. He loved her, but he'd never be good enough for her. She deserved someone who was her equal financially, and someone who didn't let her down when she needed them most. Unlike him, the screwup who couldn't keep it together no matter how much he tried or prayed.

Julia flung her purse and keys on the coffee table, and walked through her empty apartment to her bedroom. She threw herself face down on her bed. Billie had gone to the gym this morning, and had firm lunch plans. She should have the apartment to herself for a little longer.

She scrunched her eyes closed, losing the battle to hold back more tears. The events of the morning plagued her mind. She thought she'd been prepared for anything, imagined all sorts of scenarios. But she hadn't been ready to hear the devastating news her birth mother had fired at her this morning.

Why hadn't Sean gotten his act together? He'd known how important that meeting had been for her. It could have been so easy to pick him up on the way, to have him sitting beside her as she'd tried to digest everything she'd learned about her birth mother.

Sean had proved he couldn't be trusted to keep his word. He made empty promises, not taking the necessary steps to ensure he could fulfill his obligations. Why hadn't he told her earlier that he couldn't afford to fix his Jeep? Did he worry that she'd reject him because he was struggling financially?

How could she embark on a relationship with a man she couldn't depend on? If only he'd shared his financial problems with her and not taken a risk by relying on his broken Jeep to get to the café today. It hurt too much when the people she loved let her down.

Exhausted, she rolled over on her back and stared at the ceiling through watery lashes. *Lord, why did this have to happen? I hate how Amanda is so hard and bitter, and she doesn't even acknowledge Your existence. Please open her eyes and heart to the truth.*

She buried her face in her pillow, her labored breathing starting to calm. She trusted God, and her faith had a firm foundation. God kept His promises, and she could rely on Him to look after her. And look after her birth mother. She prayed she'd have enough time and opportunity to build some kind of meaningful relationship with Amanda before it was too late.

The intercom in Sean's apartment buzzed, and he struggled to his feet. He turned down the volume on the ball game on television, glad the interruption had come during the halftime break.

He rubbed his hand over his face. Who could be waiting downstairs? The buzzer pealed again. Someone was impatient. He couldn't imagine it was Julia, not after what had happened earlier today.

What a disaster! He'd spent the afternoon berating himself for messing up this morning. He'd switched on the ball game as a distraction, to try to help him forget about how he'd hurt her.

He pressed the intercom button. "Hello."

"Hi, it's Gemma. Can I come up?"

He exhaled. What did she want? He thought he'd made it clear that he wasn't interested in seeing her again.

"You there, Sean?"

"Yeah."

"You letting me in or what?"

"Okay." It was easier to talk in the hall rather than outside on the street, especially if her family's goons were following her around.

He unlocked the security door downstairs. Gemma would be on his doorstep within minutes. Doubts filled his mind. What was she up to? Why the sudden interest in seeing him? Not that he planned to invite Gemma inside. He'd talk at the door before sending her on her way.

Grateful he was dressed in decent clothes, he glanced around the living room. He had tidied up after lunch, directing his frustration over this morning into cleaning up the apartment. His phone was still missing, despite doing what he considered a thorough search of the apartment.

He opened his apartment door. The elevator ground to a halt on his floor, and he heard the sliding doors open. Gemma appeared, carrying a hot pink suitcase. She tottered down the plush carpeted hall on four-inch heels, dragging the compact suitcase behind her.

Her smile widened. "I'm so glad you're home. I wasn't sure if you'd be here."

He stood in the doorway, one shoulder leaning against the frame. "You could've called me first." And he could have talked her out of wasting her time visiting him.

"It's okay." She halted in front of him.

"What's up? Why do you need to see me?"

She flicked her blond locks behind her ears. "Can we talk inside your apartment?"

He crossed his arms over his chest. "Why?" He nodded toward her case. "Are you going somewhere?"

She giggled. "Yeah, you know me. Always on the move. My feet are killing me, so if we can chat inside…"

He blew out a sigh and stepped back. She wasn't going to take no for an answer. Better to talk inside, and get this over with as soon as possible.

She walked past him, stashing her case beside the sofa before sinking into the plush cushions. "Nice place you have here."

"It's Ryan's apartment."

"Cool. Oh, am I interrupting the game?" She kicked off her heels. "We can watch the game and talk later." She helped herself to a handful of potato crisps from a small bowl on the coffee table.

He frowned. "What's going on? What do you want?"

She finished munching on the chips. "Do you mind if I grab a soda? I didn't have time to stop for lunch."

"You're stalling. I want to know right now what's up with you."

"Calm down." She patted his arm and strolled past him to the kitchen. "There's no rush. I have no plans for the rest of the day."

He followed her into the kitchen. "Well, I do. I'm playing guitar at a charity concert tonight."

"Really." She popped the lid on the can of soda and took a big swig. "Ah, that's better. Thanks for the drink."

He shrugged. "Spill it."

"What, the drink?"

"Stop playing games. Tell me the truth."

Her shoulders slumped. "I need somewhere to crash for a few days."

"What? You think you can stay here?"

"Why not? I assume you have a spare room."

He shook his head. "No way. You need to leave now."

"Here's the thing." She twirled a lock of hair around her finger. "I need to lie low for a few days, and no one would think to look for me here."

"Gemma, what have you done? No, don't tell me. I don't want to get involved."

"It's no biggie. Everything will blow over in a few days. I can hole up here, check out your DVD collection—"

"No!" He paced the length of his kitchen. "I'm not saving you this time. Go check into a hotel or something."

Her mouth trembled and she reached for his hand. "Sean, please. Just this once."

He stepped back, shaking his hand out of her grasp. "You need to leave now. Right now."

She pouted. "Can I at least make a sandwich before you boot me out?"

"Okay, make a sandwich. Then you must go, and find somewhere else to stay tonight." He leaned against the kitchen counter.

She found a jar of peanut butter in his pantry cupboard.

He let out a deep breath. Ten minutes, fifteen at the most, and she should be gone. Hopefully, this time for good.

Chapter 16

Julia flung her gym bag onto the passenger seat of her car and slid into the driver's seat. After the terrible morning she'd experienced, a boxing class at the gym was what she needed to get rid of her excess stress before the charity-concert performance tonight.

Her car keys slipped through her fingers, her shaky hands missing the ignition slot. She fumbled on the floor near her feet, her hand brushing over smooth leather.

Sean's wallet. She stashed it in her gym bag. He must have left it in her car this morning.

She gulped in a few shallow breaths. His apartment was now her next stop. She had no choice. He'd need his license before tonight if his car started and he planned to drive to the concert. Plus, he needed his cash and other personal items.

Minutes later, she drove out of her street on her way to Sean's place. She had enough time to drop off his wallet before her boxing class. He must not realize his wallet was missing, otherwise he would have contacted her. That was assuming he'd found his phone and could locate her phone number.

She sighed, slowing to negotiate the Saturday-afternoon pedestrian traffic around Manly Wharf. It was a beautiful day for a ferry ride, and Manly was full of tourists enjoying a day outdoors in the sunshine.

She drove up the eastern hill and parked outside Sean's apartment building. He was the last person she wanted to see this afternoon. Anger and disappointment over this morning's fiasco with her birth mother simmered in her mind. Why had she ever believed she could rely on him?

She walked to the apartment building entrance and ran into Sean's father. What was he doing here?

"Hi, Julia," Brian said.

She smiled. "Hey, Brian. Can I ask a favor? Sean left his wallet in my car this morning, and my gym class starts soon. Can you please take this up to Sean for me?"

He drew his bushy eyebrows together. "You're not staying? I was hoping you could stay for a little while, and I'm sure Sean would want to see you."

He unlocked the security door and held it open, leaving Julia no choice but to follow him inside.

"I really must get going soon," she said.

He pushed the elevator button and the door slid open. "Come on up. I want to ask you something."

"Oh." She stepped into the elevator.

"How's Sean doing? He seems to be well and staying out of trouble."

She nodded. "He's doing great at work, and he's starting an IT course next week."

He smiled. "That's good news. I'm glad he has finally left his old life behind and is making a fresh start."

The elevator door opened, and she walked with him along the short hall to Sean's apartment.

Brian knocked on the door. "I could use my key, but I'm hoping he's home."

She nodded. If Sean was out, she could leave the wallet with his father and disappear to her boxing class. She'd see Sean tonight, and by then she'd have more time to get her head together, and process the events of this morning.

* * *

A knock sounded on his front door. Sean frowned. Who could it be? Maybe one of his elderly neighbors.

Gemma finished the last bite of her sandwich. "Can I get the door?"

"No, I'll get it."

Sean opened the door, and his jaw sagged. His father stood in the hall, suitcase and computer bag propped up against the wall. And Julia stood behind him, decked out in cute gym clothes that highlighted her trim figure.

Julia's eyes widened, most likely at Gemma, who now stood behind him.

Great, talk about bad timing. "Hey, Dad, Julia."

Julia stepped forward, thrusting his wallet into his hand. "Um, I can see you're busy, but I thought you'd need this. I must go." She spun around and rushed for the elevator.

"Julia, wait! I can explain."

She paused, her face downcast. "I'm running late for my gym class. Brian, will I see you with Sean later?"

His father nodded. "I'll be at the concert tonight."

"Good, I'll see you there." She lifted her head, her tempestuous gaze scouring over him. "We can talk after."

"Definitely." At least she was prepared to talk to him tonight. "See you at the concert."

Julia waited for the elevator, her expression grim. The sliding door opened and she stepped inside.

Sean turned to his father. "I wasn't expecting you until tomorrow."

His father's frown morphed into a scowl. "I can see that. Sean, what's going on here?"

"Hi, I'm Gemma." She stepped around Sean, offering her hand to his father.

His father narrowed his eyes, ignoring Gemma's out-stretched hand. "What's she doing here?"

"She's leaving now," Sean said.

Gemma dropped her hand and pouted. "But, Sean—"

"No." He crossed his arms over his chest, bracing for battle. "You need to leave right now. Why don't you contact your aunt in Bondi?"

She pressed her lips together. "I'd prefer not to."

"Maybe you don't have a choice." He switched his attention to his father. "Dad, how come you're here today?"

"I did leave a message on your phone this morning. Your mother thought it would be a good idea if I went to your concert tonight."

"That makes sense." His missing phone had caused him more grief, and he still hadn't found the wretched thing. It must be hidden somewhere in his apartment, but he had looked everywhere.

His father strode ahead into the apartment, coming to a halt beside Gemma's suitcase. "Is she staying here, too?"

"No, of course not."

His father's gaze swept over Gemma.

Sean cringed. Barefoot and holding a can of soda, Gemma looked at home.

She huffed. "Okay, I'm going."

Sean nodded. "Thank you."

She slipped on her heels and grabbed her suitcase. "I'll be in touch."

He shook his head. "That's not a good idea."

She ran her fingertips along his forearm. "See you later." She blew him a kiss and sashayed out the door.

His father shoved his hands on his hips. "Son, you have some explaining to do."

Sean braced for his father's onslaught. It would be

asking too much for his dad to give him the benefit of the doubt.

Brian shook his head. "I can't believe it. Why are you entertaining girls here?"

He let out a big breath. "She'd only just arrived, and I was booting her out when you turned up."

"Do you think I'm stupid? She made her agenda with you very clear."

"It's not how it seems. Dad, you have to believe me."

"Then why invite her in? She looked very comfortable here. Too comfortable. And what about Julia?"

Sean rubbed his hands over his face. "I've messed everything up with her."

"I warned you not to get involved with Julia. But you never listen to me—"

"Now, wait a minute. Julia was angry with me before she saw Gemma here. It's a long story, and I'm going to try to straighten everything out tonight."

His father frowned. "I hope you can, but if you cheat on Julia—"

"No! I'd never cheat on Julia. I may have done a lot of bad stuff in the past, but never that." Sean counted to three, attempting to calm his rising temper. "Gemma wanted to stay, but I said no. The truth is, she's in some kind of trouble, and I'm not bailing her out this time."

"This time." His father shook his head. "I hate to think what happened between the two of you last time."

"It's a long and complicated story."

"How do you know this girl?"

"We met in Melbourne."

"Oh." Brian walked toward the window, staring at the harbor view. "Does she have some kind of hold over you?"

"Not exactly." Sean sank into the sofa and dropped his

head in his hands. He had no option but to tell his father the truth, and pray he'd cope. "I owed her uncle money."

"What?" His dad whirled around. "How did this happen?"

"Gambling debts, mainly."

His father's face glowed red in the afternoon sunlight. "What gambling debts? Why don't I know anything about this?"

He stared at the floor, unwilling to meet his father's heated gaze. "Ryan sorted it out, and I asked him not to tell you or Mom. Mom didn't need any more stress."

"Is this why you were beaten up?"

"Yes. I was running from them when I contacted Ryan." He looked up. "I did a lot of things I now regret."

His father puffed out his chest. "How do I know you're telling the truth, when I turn up a day early and find that girl here with her suitcase?"

He stood. "Look, Dad, I don't know how I can convince you that you're wrong. You're determined to think and believe the worst-case scenario."

His father shook his head. "I'm trying. I want to believe you really are a changed man. I want to believe that you won't disappoint your mother and break her heart."

"It's true, Dad. My faith is helping me to stay on track. I promise you. I'm a different person now."

His dad cleared his throat. "I'm prepared to believe the incident with that girl is innocent, and move on."

"Thank you." He stretched out his body on the sofa, trying to relieve the tension cramping his back and neck muscles. "Today has been a horrible day, and it's not over yet. I need to get ready for the concert."

His dad nodded. "Sure. I'll settle in, and we can talk more about this over an early dinner in Manly before the concert. Unless you're planning to go with Julia?"

"She's making her own way there. The concert should be good fun." He hoped Julia had been able to think through what had happened this morning and start to process the implications of her birth mother's revelations.

He closed his eyes. What did he need to do to prove she could trust him again?

Lord, I thank You that Dad is trying to have an open mind. Please help us to reach an understanding, and help Julia to give me another chance.

Chapter 17

Julia waited behind the stage, searching the crowd for Sean. They were scheduled to perform in half an hour, and had arranged to meet at seven. The concert had commenced at six-thirty. A school choir moved into position on the stage.

She straightened the collar of her warm red jacket and smoothed down the front of her long black skirt. Where was Sean? She struggled to digest the enormity of the information she'd gleaned from her birth mother this morning. Her boxing class had helped her manage a portion of her emotions.

More tears threatened and she blinked, holding them back. At least she had an excuse tonight to wear a lot of makeup, hiding her puffy eyes and blotchy complexion.

"Julia!" Sean strode toward her, gripping his guitar case, a tentative smile hovering on his lips. "I'm here on time."

She nodded. "Is your car fixed?"

"Not yet. I was going to walk, but since Dad's here, I caught a lift with him."

"Has your father sprung another surprise visit on you?"

"Not exactly. He left a message on my phone this morning. My dad found the phone in my pantry an hour ago, partly hidden by a jar of peanut butter."

"Oh." The missing phone. One of the reasons he'd turned up late this morning. "Was the battery in your phone dead?"

He nodded. "I'm sorry. If I could turn back time and start the day over again…"

She nibbled on her lower lip. "For so many reasons, I wish I'd never started searching for my birth mother."

"You've learned the truth, and you're not going to spend the rest of your life wondering what-if."

Her throat constricted. "But the truth hurts."

His eyes softened. "Do you want to see her again?"

She nodded. "I need to finish what I started. I doubt we'll have time to build a close relationship, if that was ever an option. I'd like at least one more opportunity to talk about my faith with her."

He reached for her hand, twining his finger with hers. "I think you're brave to revisit that conversation."

"What do I have to lose?"

"It sounded as if she was firm in her views. She may not be receptive to a conversation about your faith."

"I don't want to see her die with no hope."

"What if it's a deal breaker? She may walk away from you altogether if you push the issue."

She pressed her lips together. "It's too important to ignore, and it has eternal consequences. She's living on borrowed time. I don't know how long she has left."

"You'd be wise to tread gently. I remember when Cassie first mentioned her faith, and I was not in a place where I was willing to listen to anything she had to say."

She sighed. "Amanda's heart is hardened. She was so matter-of-fact in her acceptance of her fate. It was scary."

"You said she's a counselor. She's probably spent years working through all her emotional stuff."

"But I still can't accept it. It's not fair. How could God let this happen?"

He frowned. "We live in a broken world, and we sometimes make bad choices. Our relationships are messy and complicated."

"I know." She blinked away a few stray tears. "I need time to sort myself out. I feel like my world was tipped upside down today."

He let go of her hand. "In many ways it was, and I'm sorry I added to your stress this morning."

She attempted a smile. "Can we talk more about this later?"

"You mean talk about us?"

She nodded. "My head is too full of stuff right now to think straight. I need time to pray, to get past my anger with God—"

"Seriously? You're angry with God?"

"I admit it. I'm ticked off over my situation with my birth mother. I'm so disappointed that I can't make sense of anything."

He raised an eyebrow. "But I always thought of you as calm and in control, with everything all worked out."

She stepped closer to him, lowering her voice. "Today has taught me I don't have it all together. I'm just as broken and wretched as everyone else."

He glanced over her shoulder and caught hold of her arm. "That's our cue. We need to get ready."

He lifted his guitar case off the ground and walked beside her to the stage.

The shame of her behavior earlier today couldn't be ignored. She'd made a fool of herself on the street, had almost been run over by a car. She'd yelled, ranted and behaved like a madwoman.

She'd looked down on Sean since Cassie and Ryan's

wedding, thinking she was better than him. Who was she kidding?

She stood with Sean at the edge of the stage. A sea of people filled the oval, and the bright overhead lights shone down on the crowd.

Their names were announced over the loudspeaker, and she shuffled behind Sean onto the stage. Nervous butterflies flitted in her stomach. She took a final sip from her bottled water and stood in the spotlight behind the microphone.

Sean plugged in his guitar, and then started playing the intro.

Okay, Lord, this is it. Please help me to honor You, and bring You glory as I sing tonight.

The spotlight on her intensified, obscuring her vision and view of the audience. She closed her eyes for a moment and sang. The words flowed from her mouth like rich honey, soothing her wounded soul. If only her birth mother were here tonight, listening to the powerful and redemptive words in the old hymn.

She looked up, the distant stars cloaked by the cloudy sky. An incredible sense of peace pervaded her heart. She felt as though she'd come home, as if her heavenly father had wrapped his arms around her, cocooning her from the harsh blows of life.

She sang the final notes, a few tears trickling from beneath her lashes. Her blinders had been removed. She was no longer ignorant to the harsh reality of her own life choices, and she could see how her own behavior had impacted Sean.

He held her hand, his grip firm and reassuring. Together they acknowledged the fervent applause from the audience.

Her mouth broke into a broad smile. Something had

shifted in her world today, changing her outlook and perspective.

"Thank You, Lord," she whispered. Tonight she had been blessed.

Sean held Julia's hand and guided her off the stage. She looked dazed, as if the spotlights on the stage had blinded her vision. Her exquisite voice had touched his heart. The audience had hushed during the song, mesmerized by her performance.

When he reached his gear behind the stage, he let go of her hand. Leaning forward, he packed up his guitar in the case. "We did really well tonight."

She nodded. "That was an amazing experience."

"You sang beautifully, as always."

"But something was different, extraspecial. You felt it, didn't you?"

He nodded. "Look, I want to be honest and explain why Gemma was at my apartment today."

She waved her hand through the air. "It doesn't matter."

He touched her shoulder. "I don't want you to get the wrong idea. She turned up on my doorstep and—"

"It's okay. I trust you. I know you'd tell me if something happened that I needed to know about."

"Really?" Hope rose in his chest, lightening his mood. Could it be true? Had he started to regain her trust?

"I'm sorry that I acted weird earlier. It's been a strange kind of day."

"Tell me about it. Do you want to have coffee? I can let Dad know I won't need a lift home."

She shook her head. "I'm exhausted, and it would be good for you to spend time with your father."

Disappointment shot through him. "Are you sure?" Was she giving him the brush-off?

"I don't know what I want to do, or what's best for me. I need to pray, seek wise counsel. If Cassie's week isn't too full, I may even fly up to Queensland and spend some time with her."

His mouth gaped. "You're going away this week? What about work? Who's going to cover your job, since I won't be there? My IT course is next week."

She shrugged her shoulders. "I don't know. Maybe I'll see Cassie on the weekend." She sighed. "I have to talk with my parents and let them know what has happened. And tell Billie. It's going to be tough, and I'll see how I feel during the week."

He frowned. "I could postpone my course—"

"No, it's important you do it. It's only a week, and I can put off a lot of work things until the following week. It will all sort itself out."

He let out a deep breath. He'd miss her, and he wished she felt more comfortable to turn to him for help and support. But it was too late now for regrets. All he could do was pray, and try to repair the damage he'd caused today.

She attempted a smile. "I'd better go."

"Sure." He swallowed hard, trying to dislodge the lump that had formed in his throat.

"Have a good week at your course."

He nodded. "Take care."

"I will." She melted into the crowd. Would she disappear from his life? Was it possible they could have a future together?

He walked to his father's car, his heart heavy. He loved Julia, and he had let her down at the worst possible time. Could she forgive him and give their relationship another chance?

His father stood beside his late-model sedan, checking his phone.

"I thought you'd be with Julia now."

Sean shook his head. "I totally messed up today."

"It can't be as bad as all that?"

"It is." He slipped into the passenger seat. "As usual, I let her down, like I've disappointed everyone else in my life."

"I don't think you're a disappointment," his father said.

He sat up straighter in his seat. "Don't joke with me. You wrote me off after I crashed your car into the creek."

His father frowned and switched on the car engine. "You were driving drunk. You were also under the legal age to drink in the first place. You could have killed yourself or someone else."

Shame rippled through him. "I made a mistake. I admit I was stupid and made dumb decisions. But you always expected me to mess up. I could never please you."

His father's frown deepened, and he reversed the sedan out of the parking space. "I'm not apologizing for my attitude back then. Face it, Sean, when did you give me a reason to believe in you?"

"When did you give me a chance to try? Nothing I ever did was good enough for you."

They drove in silence. His father parked his car in a visitor space at the front of Sean's apartment complex.

Sean unclicked his seat belt.

His father brushed his hand over his thinning gray hair. "You were the kid that never grew up, getting into trouble as soon as you started walking. I always thought your mother was too soft on you, gave you too many chances."

"Mom loved me." Sean's voice trembled. "I wanted your love, too. And your attention. Ryan was your golden boy, still is. It's like I was in the way, an annoyance…"

His father banged his fist against the steering wheel. "How can you say this? I did my best. You're my son."

"You sold the farm. The farm I wanted to run for you and keep in the family."

His father froze for a few moments. "You really wanted the commitment and responsibility of looking after the farm?"

Sean nodded. "I told you I'd get my act together, become more responsible. But you didn't believe me, didn't trust me enough to let me do it." Bitterness laced his voice. "I know your dream was for Ryan to take it over."

His father shook his head. "Ryan didn't want it. He had grand plans to make his mark in the business world. I didn't think you were serious about settling down, especially after the incident with the car. And there were other factors to consider."

"What things? I thought it was because you distrusted me."

"It's much more complicated." His father pressed his lips together. "Your mother had a cancer scare."

Sean's hands trembled. "No. Not Mom."

His father sighed. "It's true."

"What? When? Why didn't you tell me about this?"

"Remember years ago, when we had to keep driving into Bathurst for regular appointments?"

He nodded. "Wasn't that farm business?"

His father shook his head. "The treatments your mother received worked, and the tests eventually came back clear. During that time, our neighbors inherited some money and offered us an excellent price for the farm. An offer we couldn't refuse, and much higher than I had anticipated we could receive."

His father's words spun in his mind. "So you took their offer and retired."

"Yes. I spent years working the farm from dawn to dusk, building up the livestock and trying to earn a decent living despite droughts and other disasters. Your mother's illness was a wake-up call, and we made the decision to take the money and retire."

"It wasn't about me? You weren't punishing me by selling the farm?"

"No, and I'm sorry. We had no idea you believed this. I admit I've favored Ryan over the years, which was wrong. But our decision to sell the farm wasn't about you or Ryan."

Sean nodded. Everything made sense now. He'd misjudged his father, holding a grudge over something that didn't exist. Compassion shone in his father's eyes, and deep down he knew the man was telling the truth.

"Dad, I'm sorry I gave you so much grief. Why didn't you tell us about Mom's illness?"

"Ryan was studying in the city and we didn't want to burden him. And you were…"

"I know. Out of control in so many ways, lost and looking for meaning in my life in all the wrong places."

"Sean, I'm sorry our decision hurt you. That was never our intention."

He nodded. "Can we start over, wipe the slate clean?"

"Of course. Sitting here, talking to you tonight, I can see how much you've changed. And grown up. I'm proud of the achievements you've made, and I hope you can work things out with Julia."

"Thanks, Dad. I appreciate your support." He opened the door and stepped out of the car. A new day would dawn tomorrow, and he was no longer burdened with the family baggage from his past.

Lord, thank You for forgiving me. Thank You for giving me the courage to talk with Dad and resolve our issues.

He walked up the path to the entrance of his apartment building with his father, his step light. Now, if only he could sit down and sort everything out with Julia... She was hurting, and he feared she wasn't going to be as easy to convince as his father.

He understood her need for space, her desire to process her birth mother's bombshells and break the news to her parents and sister. How could he prove to Julia that he loved her and would do his best to not disappoint her again?

A week and a half later, Julia arrived at work Monday midmorning. Her early flight from Queensland had been delayed. She had rushed to the church office straight from the airport, her luggage in tow.

Sean sat at her desk, eyebrows raised. "I heard you've been soaking up the sun in Queensland."

She nodded. "I'm sorry I'm late. My flight was rescheduled. You've been talking to Ryan."

"Cassie, actually."

"Oh." She'd spent the weekend with Cassie and Ryan at the resort, relaxing and taking stock of her life. She had a few big decisions to make, tough decisions in many ways. "I'll stash my suitcase out back, and I'll be ready to start work soon."

Sean stood. "No, let me help you."

"It's okay. I need to freshen up anyway."

He smiled. "You look great."

"Thanks, I feel a lot better." She glanced at her watch. "I'm already half an hour late, and I promised Billie I'd have lunch with her. I should get moving."

"It's okay, don't rush. I have everything under control."

"I can see that. How was your course?"

"Good. I learned some helpful stuff."

"I'm glad."

"Do you have plans after work?"

She shook her head.

"Why don't we have fish and chips at the beach for dinner, if the wind isn't too cold?"

She smiled. "Sure. I'm going home for lunch, and I'll grab a warmer jacket."

"Sounds great. I have a lot to tell you."

"Me, too. I've had time to think and work out a whole lot of stuff." She flicked her fingers through her hair, which hung loose around her shoulders. "But we're not getting paid to chat, so I'd better get moving. I have Friday's work to catch up on, as well."

He nodded, his eyes sparkling. "We have all evening to talk. I can wait."

"Yes." She picked up the handle of her suitcase and dragged it along the carpeted hallway. She felt invigorated from her time away, and looked forward to seeing Sean after work. But first she must talk to Billie. And try to smooth over the issues that had arisen between them since she had made contact with her birth mother.

Chapter 18

At lunchtime, Julia retrieved her suitcase from an empty office out back. Her phone beeped, and she checked her messages. Billie was collecting her in five minutes from the street around the corner from the church.

She waved goodbye to Sean. He lounged back in her seat at her desk, phone cradled between his shoulder and ear.

She smiled and headed outside into the warm winter sunshine. Her heart felt lighter today, and she was glad to see Sean at home at her desk this morning. She'd missed him more than she'd thought she would.

Somehow, he'd crept into her heart and taken up residence there, and she yearned to make things right with him. If that was possible. She could understand if he'd had enough of her problems, and decided to walk away from their relationship.

Billie pulled up at the curb. Julia stashed her suitcase on the backseat and slid into the front seat beside her sister.

"Hey, Billie. Thanks for the ride."

"No problem. I was thinking we could order in tonight. I want to hear all about your trip."

She tucked her hair behind her ears. "Well, actually, I'm seeing Sean tonight."

Billie's smile widened. "That's great news. Does this

mean you've fixed everything with your gorgeous surfer boy?"

"Stop calling him that."

"But it's true. I really like him, and you'd be crazy to let him slip through your fingers."

She perched her sunglasses on her nose. "I guess I'll wait and see what happens tonight. I've had time to think and work out what I want. But he might have different ideas than mine."

Her sister shook her head and parked her car in the garage under their apartment complex. "The boy loves you and you love him. It's that simple."

Julia hoped Billie was right. She dragged her suitcase upstairs behind her sister, who carried a delicious smelling bag of Asian takeout food.

Billie opened the door to their apartment. "I hope you feel like laksa."

Her mouth watered. "I sure do." She set the table, grabbed two sodas from the fridge and offered a blessing before they started their meal.

Billie sipped her soup using her plastic spoon. "Delish, and just the right amount of chili."

She smiled. "Thanks for picking up lunch."

"You're welcome. My last appointment before lunch cancelled, giving me extra time to get organized."

Julia tasted her prawn laksa, the chili in the coconut-milk soup exploding in her mouth. Her taste buds tingled. "I've been doing a lot of thinking about the situation with my birth mother."

Her sister lifted a brow. "You're still mad at me?"

She shook her head. "I can understand why you think I'm being too hard on her, and judgmental."

"You can't blame her for not being the perfect biological mother. Just because she didn't live up to your expectations…"

"I know. And she could have chosen to remain anonymous, avoiding this situation altogether."

Billie paused, her spoon midair. "It's a tough situation, and I can't imagine it was easy for her to see you again. Sean is right. If you get the bright idea to try to shove religion down her throat—"

"I'd never do that. And I can't even remember the last time you regularly attended church."

"Touché. I have my own private beliefs."

Julia frowned. That was what Billie always said. Her faith was a private matter she didn't like talking about with anyone.

What had happened to her sister? Why had Billie turned her back on the church? Billie had been very involved with their youth group and a regular church attender in her teens.

No matter how Julia broached the subject, her sister refused to bite and talk about her faith. Julia prayed for her sister, that she didn't lose her way with her lone ranger approach. One day, she hoped Billie would open up and talk with her.

Julia swallowed a flavorsome mouthful of soft noodles. "This is good. By the way, I wrote a letter to my birth mom while I was in Queensland."

"Really?" Her sister leaned forward in her seat. "What did you say?"

"I kept it low-key. I said I was glad we'd met and I'd like to meet again for coffee, if that works for her."

Billie smiled. "Jules, I'm proud of you. I know how difficult it would have been for you to write that letter."

"It was Cassie who helped me. I'm also thinking about pulling out of the missionary recruitment process and staying in Australia. I don't know how long Amanda has left, and I can always explore the missionary opportunities later."

Her sister wrinkled her nose. "I've no idea why you'd want to live in a primitive country without the comforts of home. I hope you won't be moving overseas anytime soon. I'd miss you."

"Can you forgive me for yelling at you earlier?" They'd had a heated conversation regarding her birth mother before she flew to Queensland.

"Of course. You're my sister. By the way, I've spoken with Mom, and she's coming to terms with your news."

"Thank you. I'm going to see her and Dad tomorrow."

"Mom will be thrilled to hear you're staying in the country."

She smiled. "Have you heard any news about your search for your birth parents?"

Billie shook her head, tears glistening in her eyes. "I fear I'm going to hear bad news."

"I'm praying you'll hear something soon."

Her sister nodded. "I hope God is listening."

She frowned. Billie rarely talked about God, and her despondent tone was out of character. She needed to keep praying that her sister's search for her birth parents would be fruitful, and not weaken her faith.

And she needed to pray about seeing Sean tonight. *Lord, please help me to say what's in my heart, to be open and honest about everything. And help me to listen to Sean and resolve our issues.*

Later in the day, Julia locked the church office's sliding door and followed Sean into the courtyard. The sun was setting on the western horizon, rich hues of pink, red and orange coloring the cloudy sky.

Sean drew his eyebrows together. "We're going to be having a twilight dinner and miss the sunset."

"I'm sorry we're late. Between my flight delay this morning and catching up from Friday, I had a lot of work to get through."

"It's okay. I'm just happy to be with you."

"Me, too. Dinner sounds great." She slipped her hand into his, and they walked together on the sidewalk. The crowds of tourists had thinned along The Corso. She turned up the collar of her jacket, the wind off the ocean billowing down the pedestrian thoroughfare.

"I think we'd better eat at a café," Sean said. "Otherwise, we'll get blown away in this gale-force wind."

"Sure. Why don't we walk around to Shelley Beach? We have time to get there, and the path is well lit for our walk back after dark."

"I'm in. After staring at a computer screen all day, the exercise will do me good."

They walked in companionable silence, reaching the promenade opposite the ocean. Waves pounded the sand, sending a spray of seawater up in the air and over the rocks at the headland.

Her heart rate quickened. Sean's warm hand, entwined with hers, inspired thoughts of settling down, and making his presence in her life a more permanent arrangement. How could she make everything right between them?

He stepped closer, his arm brushing against hers. "What are you thinking?"

She paused at the white-painted wooden railing, swallowing the lump that had formed in her throat. "I'm thinking that I've been a fool, blinded to my own faults while I sat in judgment on others."

His eyes widened. "I don't follow. I don't think you're judgmental."

She swiped her hair off her face, her ponytail whipping around her neck in the gusty breeze. "That's because you can't see the truth in my heart, the pride I've hidden away all too well."

"Yeah, but you don't act like a snob or anything." He stared out at the ocean, the sky lit up in bright hues. "I can't see how this is a big deal."

She straightened her spine. It was time to tell him the truth. "I hate to admit it, but I judged you as not worthy of me. I was wrong, very wrong."

Sean chuckled. "The irony of your confession is you've always treated me much better than my own flesh and blood. I'm not proud of some of the things I did in the past, and frankly, I can't blame you if you were suspicious or wary of me."

"It's more than that." She frowned, searching for the right words to express her feelings. "I was shattered when I discovered my birth mother's history. I had trouble believing and accepting her life choices, which were foreign to my own life experiences. She doesn't have a clue who my father is."

He nodded. "She lived a rough life that has unfortunately caught up with her. I'm so sorry her health isn't good."

"Billie and I had a fight over Amanda just before I left for Queensland."

He raised an eyebrow. "Really? I thought your sister was supportive of your decisions."

"Not this time." She looked down at the path. A row of ants circled an ice cream cone that had been spilled earlier in the day. "Billie dished out some tough love that I didn't appreciate at the time."

"That was gutsy of her."

"Yep. She told me to stop sulking, to accept my birth

mother for who she was, or walk away." She stared into his warm eyes. "And if I couldn't accept her, I was a hypocrite who'd forgotten about the concept of unconditional love."

"Wow, she didn't hold anything back."

Julia nodded. "It was what I needed to hear. Mom and Dad were my soft landing, giving me lots of love and support. But Billie gave me the kick in the pants I needed to move forward."

"I can't imagine how difficult it must be to have finally found her, and then discover she's dying."

"It has totally changed my whole outlook on life, and helped me to make some hard decisions about the future."

"What does this mean for us?" He held both her hands, looking deep into her eyes. "Julia, I love you. I'd like to think you'll give us a chance to see if we can have a future together."

She stood on tiptoes, dropping a light kiss on his lips. "I love you, Sean. I now know I'm no better than anyone else, and I'm sorry I gave you a hard time over your car breaking down." She lowered her lashes, her lips trembling. "You do one thing wrong, and I crucify you."

He blotted a tear on her cheek with the pad of his finger. "Please don't cry." He tipped her head up. "I understand why you went off at me. You were under a lot of stress, and I deserved it. I let you down when you needed me most. I deserved your judgment and condemnation."

She wrapped her arms around his waist, snuggling her cheek into the collar of his jacket. "Please forgive me. I've been such an idiot."

"Of course I'll forgive you." He stepped back, smiling. "Let's keep moving before we're drowned by the waves crashing on the rocks."

She strolled next to him along the path, mesmerized

by the rolling surf that was in sync with the accelerated beat of her heart. "I now get what the 'Amazing Grace' hymn is all about."

"Huh." He slowed his pace, his gaze curious.

"I understand the importance of God's grace, and how we've all failed and can't be good enough for God, no matter how hard we try."

"You've had a strong faith for years. When I came to faith, I was so broken I had no doubt that I needed a savior. Grace made sense to me, because I knew for sure I definitely wasn't good enough for God."

"You see, that's the thing. I've always thought of myself as a good person. I tried to obey the Ten Commandments, and follow all the teachings in the Bible. I had accepted Jesus as my savior without really acknowledging the true extent of my imperfections." She frowned. "Does this make any sense?"

He nodded. "I've been in and out of trouble for most of my life, and I knew I was a rotten sinner. The old hymn, 'Amazing Grace,' says it all."

"It was while I was singing at the concert that I finally started to get it. I didn't need to marry a pastor to please God or improve my status in God's eyes. It's as if God opened my eyes to see the truth."

"Wow. So much has happened in your life in the past few weeks."

"I know." She stepped onto the dry sand at Shelley Beach, gazing at the long stretch of beach from Manly to Queenscliff. The sinking sun lit up the clouds in the sky in a kaleidoscope of bright colors.

"A beautiful sunset," she said.

He smiled. "And a beautiful girl." He kissed the tip of her nose before dropping his gaze to her mouth and claiming her lips.

She wound her arms around his shoulders, and ran her fingers through his silky, windswept hair. He deepened the kiss, and her heart melted.

Sean drew back, his expression serious. "Where do we go from here?"

"I've made the decision to stay in Sydney, and I'm pulling out of the missionary recruitment process."

"Why? I thought that was your dream."

"Finding my birth mom sealed my decision."

He frowned. "But I thought you wanted to commit your life to full-time missionary work overseas."

She shrugged her shoulders. "I've learned it's not about what I want. I need to seek God's will, not try to make the things I want happen. I have to trust that God will take care of me."

He grinned. "You know I'm serious about us, and our relationship. I'm so happy to hear you're staying in Sydney."

"I thought you would be."

His smile widened. "I want to build a life with you. I think it's too soon to talk about marriage, but that's the direction my thoughts are heading."

Her heart overflowed with joy. "Yes, me, too. We don't need to rush. I love you, and I want to be with you."

"I promise you, the next time you arrange to see your birth mother, I'll be there if you want me there."

"Yes, and I'll personally collect you from your apartment to make sure you're there on time."

He sneaked a kiss. "I like the idea of you chauffeuring me around."

She laughed. "You need to get the money together for a new starter motor."

"It's all good. I've booked the Jeep in for a service next week, and they've ordered the part."

"I'm glad to hear this."

"Why don't you come out with us in the van next weekend? Do some mission work at home?"

"It sounds interesting. Is this the group who sponsored the charity concert?"

"Yes. They work with homeless people, feed them and talk with them. It's a lot of hard work, but also rewarding to know you're helping others."

She wound her fingers through his. "Tell me more. Maybe this is the kind of thing I could do."

"All I know is that I believe we were brought together for a reason. I'm so glad I met you when I did, after I'd cleaned up my act."

She nodded. "I'm praying for us, that our relationship will be blessed."

"Same here. All my dreams are starting to come true."

Her heart skipped a beat. "I can't wait to discover what lies ahead for us."

Chapter 19

Eighteen months later

Julia stood with her father inside the main entrance to Beachside Community Church. Billie adjusted the delicate bridal veil, draping it over Julia's face. Cassie fussed behind her, spreading out the train of her beaded ivory silk gown.

"You look stunning," Billie said.

She smiled. "It's really happening. I'm marrying Sean today." Their twelve-month engagement had seemed as though it was never going to end.

Billie nodded, and the upbeat tempo in the music slowed for the bridal march. "That's our cue to get moving."

Her father's eyes lit up. "Are you ready, sweetheart?"

"Let's do it." Julia linked her arm through his, and held a heavy bouquet of pale pink roses in her trembling hands. Her diamond solitaire engagement ring, a family heirloom, glimmered in the sunlight that streamed through the pretty stained glass windows.

Billie walked ahead into the church, followed by Cassie.

Her father guided her to the wide aisle in the center of the church. Familiar smiling faces, family and friends, lined the rows of seats. Work colleagues from the homeless shelter filled the back rows.

Sean had stayed on in his role in the church office, and fourteen months ago, she'd started a new position in the office of the charity organization that managed the homeless shelter.

She gasped, her gaze colliding with Sean's. He stood tall at the front of the church, decked out in a tuxedo, a big grin covering his handsome face.

Julia concentrated on keeping step with the music, glad she had her father next to her. She spotted Amanda. Her birth mother was alone, standing back from the aisle toward the middle of the church.

Tears moistened her eyes. Amanda had declined her parents' invitation to the wedding reception, but had agreed to attend the wedding ceremony.

Her difficult and complicated relationship with Amanda hadn't improved since their first meeting. Julia hoped and prayed they'd find more common ground over the coming months and form a closer bond.

She approached the front of the church and glanced to the left. Her mother looked fantastic, smiling and taking photos, clearly enjoying her mother-of-the-bride role.

Julia broke with tradition and paused, embracing her mom in a warm hug. Her mother had accepted Amanda's tumultuous arrival in her daughter's life with grace and humility.

New tears threatened to flow as her gaze reconnected with Sean's.

His eyes gleamed, full of love and promises for a long and happy future together.

Her spirit soared as she joined hands with the man she loved. A man of integrity who had earned her respect and trust.

He leaned in closer, his breath a whisper on her neck. "You look sensational."

Heat rose in her face and she squeezed his hand. "So do you."

They moved forward with her father, climbing a few steps to stand in front of Simon on the stage.

Simon quoted the love verses in Corinthians in his opening address. Her father consented to the marriage before taking a seat beside her mother. Their friends in the church band played the introduction to "Amazing Grace." Their special song.

She gazed up into Sean's vibrant eyes, in awe of the man standing in front of her who wanted to love, honor and cherish her forever.

Soon it was time to speak their vows, their sacred promises in the sight of God and their family and friends.

Sean held both of her hands, his voice strong and confident. She spoke her promises, her love for him filling her heart.

Sean slid the diamond-encrusted wedding band onto her finger, her hand shaky in his reassuring warm grasp.

She repeated her vows in a clear voice and fumbled for a moment before gliding his wedding ring over his knuckle.

Simon pronounced them husband and wife, and he gave Sean permission to kiss his bride.

Sean lifted up her veil, his eyes glittering. "The moment I've been waiting for all day."

He placed a gentle hand on her waist and lowered his head, his lips soft on her mouth. She welcomed the intimacy, and he deepened the kiss. Her mind spun in an ocean of exhilarating sensations, her body responding to her husband's loving embrace.

The congregation burst into loud applause, and he

stepped back, his gaze warming her heart. "I can't wait to have you all to myself."

"Me, either." She was a blessed woman, and couldn't wait to discover what their future held.

* * * * *

REQUEST YOUR FREE BOOKS!

2 FREE INSPIRATIONAL NOVELS
PLUS 2
FREE
MYSTERY GIFTS

Love Inspired®

REQUEST YOUR FREE BOOKS!

2 FREE INSPIRATIONAL NOVELS
PLUS 2
FREE
MYSTERY GIFTS

Love Inspired
HISTORICAL
INSPIRATIONAL HISTORICAL ROMANCE

YES! Please send me 2 FREE Love Inspired® Historical novels and my 2 FREE mystery gifts (gifts are worth about $10). After receiving them, if I don't wish to receive any more books, I can return the shipping statement marked "cancel." If I don't cancel, I will receive 4 brand-new novels every month and be billed just $4.74 per book in the U.S. or $5.24 per book in Canada. That's a savings of at least 21% off the cover price. It's quite a bargain! Shipping and handling is just 50¢ per book in the U.S. and 75¢ per book in Canada.* I understand that accepting the 2 free books and gifts places me under no obligation to buy anything. I can always return a shipment and cancel at any time. Even if I never buy another book, the two free books and gifts are mine to keep forever.

102/302 IDN F5CY

Name	(PLEASE PRINT)	

Address		Apt. #

City	State/Prov.	Zip/Postal Code

Signature (if under 18, a parent or guardian must sign)

Mail to the **Harlequin® Reader Service:**
IN U.S.A.: P.O. Box 1867, Buffalo, NY 14240-1867
IN CANADA: P.O. Box 609, Fort Erie, Ontario L2A 5X3

Want to try two free books from another series?
Call 1-800-873-8635 or visit www.ReaderService.com.

* Terms and prices subject to change without notice. Prices do not include applicable taxes. Sales tax applicable in N.Y. Canadian residents will be charged applicable taxes. Offer not valid in Quebec. This offer is limited to one order per household. Not valid for current subscribers to Love Inspired Historical books. All orders subject to credit approval. Credit or debit balances in a customer's account(s) may be offset by any other outstanding balance owed by or to the customer. Please allow 4 to 6 weeks for delivery. Offer available while quantities last.

Your Privacy—The Harlequin® Reader Service is committed to protecting your privacy. Our Privacy Policy is available online at www.ReaderService.com or upon request from the Harlequin Reader Service.

We make a portion of our mailing list available to reputable third parties that offer products we believe may interest you. If you prefer that we not exchange your name with third parties, or if you wish to clarify or modify your communication preferences, please visit us at www.ReaderService.com/consumerchoice or write to us at Harlequin Reader Service Preference Service, P.O. Box 9062, Buffalo, NY 14269. Include your complete name and address.

LIHDIR13R

REQUEST YOUR FREE BOOKS!
2 FREE RIVETING INSPIRATIONAL NOVELS
PLUS 2 FREE MYSTERY GIFTS

YES! Please send me 2 FREE Love Inspired® Suspense novels and my 2 FREE mystery gifts (gifts are worth about $10). After receiving them, if I don't wish to receive any more books, I can return the shipping statement marked "cancel." If I don't cancel, I will receive 4 brand-new novels every month and be billed just $4.74 per book in the U.S. or $5.24 per book in Canada. That's a savings of at least 21% off the cover price. It's quite a bargain! Shipping and handling is just 50¢ per book in the U.S. and 75¢ per book in Canada.* I understand that accepting the 2 free books and gifts places me under no obligation to buy anything. I can always return a shipment and cancel at any time. Even if I never buy another book, the two free books and gifts are mine to keep forever.

123/323 IDN F5AN

Name	(PLEASE PRINT)

Address	Apt. #

City	State/Prov.	Zip/Postal Code

Signature (if under 18, a parent or guardian must sign)

Mail to the Harlequin® Reader Service:
IN U.S.A.: P.O. Box 1867, Buffalo, NY 14240-1867
IN CANADA: P.O. Box 609, Fort Erie, Ontario L2A 5X3

**Are you a current subscriber to Love Inspired Suspense books
and want to receive the larger-print edition?
Call 1-800-873-8635 or visit www.ReaderService.com.**

* Terms and prices subject to change without notice. Prices do not include applicable taxes. Sales tax applicable in N.Y. Canadian residents will be charged applicable taxes. Offer not valid in Quebec. This offer is limited to one order per household. Not valid for current subscribers to Love Inspired Suspense books. All orders subject to credit approval. Credit or debit balances in a customer's account(s) may be offset by any other outstanding balance owed by or to the customer. Please allow 4 to 6 weeks for delivery. Offer available while quantities last.

Your Privacy—The Harlequin® Reader Service is committed to protecting your privacy. Our Privacy Policy is available online at www.ReaderService.com or upon request from the Harlequin Reader Service.
We make a portion of our mailing list available to reputable third parties that offer products we believe may interest you. If you prefer that we not exchange your name with third parties, or if you wish to clarify or modify your communication preferences, please visit us at www.ReaderService.com/consumerschoice or write to us at Harlequin Reader Service Preference Service, P.O. Box 9062, Buffalo, NY 14269. Include your complete name and address.

LISDIR13R

ReaderService.com

Manage your account online!

- Review your order history
- Manage your payments
- Update your address

---

*We've designed
the Harlequin® Reader Service
website just for you.*

Enjoy all the features!

- Reader excerpts from any series
- Respond to mailings and special monthly offers
- Discover new series available to you
- Browse the Bonus Bucks catalog
- Share your feedback

Visit us at:

ReaderService.com